Totally Bound Publishing books by Faith Ashlin:

Knights and Butterscotch
What You See
Pathfinder

I0570755

PATHFINDER

FAITH ASHLIN

Pathfinder
ISBN # 978-1-78430-168-2
©Copyright Faith Ashlin 2014
Cover Art by Posh Gosh ©Copyright July 2014
Interior text design by Claire Siemaszkiewicz
Totally Bound Publishing

Published in 2014 by Totally Bound Publishing, Newland House, The Point, Weaver Road, Lincoln, LN6 3QN, United Kingdom.

Totally Bound Publishing is an imprint of Total-E-Ntwined Limited.

PATHFINDER

Dedication

For Den

Chapter One

September 1941, RAF Base West Malling, 29 Squadron
0630 Hours

Bobby stood by the side of the plane, squinting as he looked up the road into the early morning sunlight, his nose crinkling up as he did so. He should put his dark glasses on, they would make life easier. He knew that. But they gave him a headache and he didn't need one, not now. He patted his pockets, just for a diversion, but he'd left his cigarettes in his room. They gave him a headache as well.

He checked the road again. He just wanted to get started.

"Watching won't make him arrive any sooner," Dennis Banister said, a smile thick in his voice. "I know how keen you are but they're right when they say a watched kettle never boils."

"It's all right for you." Bobby pulled up the collar of his flying jacket, his hands needing something to do, wishing he had that cigarette. Stamping the butt out and grinding the dregs into the ground would relieve a bit of tension. "You've got your flying partner—you're all set to go."

"But the CO says we wait until your man arrives and then we'll all start testing together."

"Yeah, but you two know each other well—you're a proper team. We'll be starting from scratch." He thrust his hands down into his pockets. Being tall meant it always felt like his jacket was riding up, even when it wasn't. He loved his RAF uniform and always felt smart and proud as soon as he slipped the jacket on. He was sure the cap made his brown hair and gray eyes look more distinguished, dependable. He turned to stare up at the airplane—so intriguing, so much potential. His fingers itched to find out what the machine could really do. "What if this guy's an idiot? What if he can't fly straight?"

"Looks like you're about to find out." Dennis nodded to the military Jeep that was just passing the guard hut at the main gate, before heading to the control room. "Are you going over to meet him?"

Bobby thought about official welcomes and Wing Commander Stockton's speech on 'only the best will do'. He'd give that a miss. "No, I'll wait here. Send him over if you see him."

"From what I've heard, this chap will be just as eager to get started as you are."

"I hope so. We need to stop sitting on our asses and start doing something useful in this goddamn war," Bobby said quietly, but with real feeling.

"Steady on, old boy." Dennis gripped Bobby's shoulder, fingers tightening for a moment before he pulled away to rest his hand on the wing of the plane. "We will, but don't rush things. This is too important to make mistakes. This little beauty could make a hell of a difference."

Bobby's eyes wandered over the Mosquito again. Not a huge plane, not like the bombers, and without the glamour of a Spitfire, but nonetheless impressive. A beautiful plane, freshly painted in a patchwork of brown and green, one that stood proud, nose held high. Her wings swept out gracefully, with two big propellers ready for action and the glass canopy that would protect her crew of two just visible. His mouth watered at the possibilities.

He was still there, still looking, twenty minutes later when he heard the sound of feet and turned to meet his new pilot—another big man, his dark blue-gray RAF uniform fitting snugly across his broad shoulders. His cap was pushed firmly onto thick dirty-blond hair, over a wide smile and brown eyes. He was tall... Really, really tall.

"Hi." A big hand was thrust in Bobby's direction. "Pilot Officer Lewis Winters, you must be Flight Lieutenant Davenport, my navigator."

"Yeah, but..." Suddenly, there were a lot of thoughts whirring around in Bobby's head. He'd deal with the most important first. "Can you actually fit inside a cockpit? Will there be room for me?"

Lewis threw his head back as he barked out a laugh, the sound catching Bobby off guard. There hadn't been much laughter around him since... For a long time. "It's a bit of a pinch, but don't worry, I've had a lot of practice. I won't squash you." Lewis' gaze made a swift journey up Bobby's body, lingering on his face. "Unless you want me to."

So it was like that, was it?

Bobby didn't mind as that was a situation he could handle. But if the guy couldn't fly, well, that was different. That he couldn't tolerate. "A lot of practice? How long have you been flying?"

"Since I was about fourteen." Lewis' gaze had gone from Bobby and was now fixed firmly on the aircraft next to them instead. "My daddy flies, back home. Local trips, crop dusting, that kind of thing. He took me up with him as soon as he could convince my mom." He slid his hands almost lovingly across the edge of a wing, moving to stand underneath, taking in every detail.

"Wait, you're from the States?"

"Yep." Lewis' accent was obvious now, the twang thick, rounded and at full throttle. "From Texas, just like you are."

"You know about me?"

"I asked around. I know a bit." Lewis started to walk around the plane, obviously checking it with a knowing eye. "Most Americans in the Royal Air Force are with the Eagle Squadrons at present, so it seems like someone high up thought it would be a good idea to put us two together."

So Bobby was paired with the new man because he was a Yank, not because he was the best. His face tightened in annoyance at the thought. The guy might be tall—very tall—with a body a man could spend a while getting to know, but none of that was important if he wasn't a great pilot. "Why aren't you in the Eagles then?"

"Because..." Lewis ran his fingertips across the fuselage, his eyes sparkling with excitement. "I wanted to get to know this baby, been requesting a transfer since I first heard about her."

"You're a fan of the Mosquito?"

"Are you kidding me?" Lewis turned to face Bobby again. "A bomber that's so fast she doesn't need to be armed, that will be in and out before the Germans even know what's hit them. And she's incredibly versatile. I reckon she could take on just about any job, you wait and see. They've already made bomber and fighter versions. I'll bet there'll be a fighter-bomber eventually. She'll be the world's fastest operational aircraft. All that and she's made of wood. Amazing."

"You know your stuff," Bobby conceded, tipping his head. "I just hope you can fly as well as you talk."

"I'll make her sing 'cause…" Lewis licked over his bottom lip, gaze locking with Bobby's, and right there, right at the back, Bobby saw a little bit of hesitancy. "She's damn near as pretty as you are." He raised his eyebrow as his face tightened and the statement was overlaid with nervousness. Bobby knew only too well why. People might be living for the moment during the war, taking chances they never would have normally — after all, the average life expectancy for a Spitfire pilot was a meager few weeks, so an airman couldn't afford to wait — but what Lewis had just done was one hell of a risk.

A man got a dishonorable discharge for homosexuality.

If a guy was that brave seemed was only right he got rewarded.

"As damn near pretty as you." Bobby pulled the steps down ready to climb up into the cockpit. "Although nowhere near as big. You want to take a look inside?"

"Hell yes." Lewis rubbed his hands together at the prospect. "Testing out this sweetheart before her first operational sortie, with you at my side — that has to be the best job anywhere in the war."

* * * *

The morning was spent going over the plane with a fine-toothed comb, first outside, then squashed together inside the small cockpit. Lewis' knowing smile had turned boyish and soft as his elbow caught Bobby. Their thighs had nowhere else to go but press together. He'd laughed out loud again when Bobby moaned as he tried to squeeze in. "Where the hell am I supposed to fit?"

They talked through every aspect with the ground crew, spent lunch arguing the Mosquito's superiority over the Spitfire. It wasn't until early afternoon that they actually got into the air.

The growl of the engines, the sharp pull up, trees disappearing below the windscreen, a barrel of pressure on the crewman's chest. A leap of faith like no other.

Lewis' excited exhalation of sound, his mumbled call of, "Yes".

After the initial rush of adrenaline, at finally — *finally* — being off the ground, and the intently focused, ingrained technical routines necessary, Bobby was determined to spend a while just watching his new pilot fly.

That was important before they got on with the real business of testing the aircraft.

Fifty minutes later he had to admit that Lewis was good. As good as the air of confidence he gave off. As good as Bobby had hoped. He seemed to be able to feel the aircraft through his fingertips, as he murmured soft requests and endearments as though she were an exotic animal, much loved but potentially lethal. Apparently Lewis learned quickly but he also seemed to instinctively know just the right moment to pull up from a dive, just how fast he could push her at each height, just how to make her engines sing sweetly.

He appeared to be in his natural environment, confident, assured and at ease, even enjoying himself. At home. At home that was, apart from the flying helmet and radio headgear that squashed his mass of hair and made his head appear a strange shape.

A while later and Bobby suddenly realized he was also being assessed. Lewis had taken difficult, complex routes, twisting and turning the plane so it was hard to follow landmarks on the ground. Deliberately trying to confuse Bobby, to get him lost.

Bobby smiled to himself. He was a first class navigator, a truly first class one. He also knew his stuff and knew how to apply that knowledge. He liked the fact that Lewis was testing him. That fact meant the guy wanted the best as well.

The Mosquito deserved no less.

* * * *

Back on the ground there was a long debriefing with Squadron Leader Roger Harris and the ground crew, where they went over the teething troubles and worked on suggestions and refinements. Then there was one last check on the plane before they were free to go and eat. Once more Lewis ran a hand tenderly over her undercarriage.

"I think we should give her a name." He smiled at Bobby, face full of enthusiasm. "She needs one, seeing she's part of the team."

"Part of the team?" Bobby raised an eyebrow but he couldn't help his lips curling in a hint of a smile.

"Yeah, you, me and… Betty. Let's call her Betty."

"Betty? That's more than a little clichéd, don't you think?"

Lewis shrugged. "I like a cliché and I have an aunt named Betty. But she should have a name as we will be trusting each other with our lives."

Bobby tipped his head in acknowledgment but he didn't lose his smile. "I have an Aunty Betty as well."

"Then Betty it is." Lewis' gaze locked with Bobby's for a brief moment. "Food?"

"Food." Bobby agreed.

Afterward they stopped at the officers' mess for a while. Lewis wrinkled his nose in disgust at the warm, dark beer. Bobby introduced him to the rest of the squadron, the names blurring in a mass of Dickies, Stans and Bills. No one cared, they all knew he'd remember them as he needed to. One of the others assured him that learning proper names was pointless — half the people had nicknames that were so ingrained, even their own mothers didn't think of them as anything else.

"You do know that the Squadron Leader's name isn't actually Roger." Dennis laughed. "He's actually called Bob."

"Then why?" Lewis pulled a confused face.

"Because he likes confusing folks when he says, 'Roger, over and out,' on the radio. He thinks he's funny."

"That's..." Lewis pulled a face.

"That's the English for you," Bobby said, laughing along with everyone else.

Coming out into the darkness, Lewis stopped and inhaled a lungful of cool night air. With his cap under his arm, his hair blew in the slight breeze. "Well." He turned to Bobby, a sudden tentativeness in his manner and voice. "Do you want to come back to my quarters?" His attention rested for a long moment on Bobby's mouth before moving up to lock their gazes. "After all, you don't want me to get lost."

"I can show you the way but I don't think there's much point in my coming in," Bobby said, already walking as Lewis scrambled to catch up.

"Why? You don't want to use the privacy to...talk?"

"Privacy?" Bobby held open the outer door to the officers' block, grinning playfully. "You don't get any privacy."

"What?"

"You're a Pilot Officer, the lowest of the low when it comes to officers. You'll be sharing with one of the other POs, if not two of them."

Lewis' face fell in a caricature of incredulous disbelief. "No?"

"Yes." The grin slipped from Bobby's face, his gaze dipping along with his voice. "I, on the other hand, am a Flight Lieutenant and as such I get a tiny room all to myself." He watched Lewis catch his breath, his tongue ghosting over his bottom lip as he clutched at his cap.

They both knew how this worked.

"You want to show me how tiny it is?" Again Lewis slid his tongue across his lip, the trail wet and shiny. He flicked his gaze up to Bobby's face and he suddenly seemed much younger than he had all day. "Please."

Bobby didn't say a word but he twisted and made his way swiftly up the stairs to the top floor, long legs making quick work of the corridor until he got to his room at the end. The door was opened as silently as possible, locked summarily behind them, then Bobby had Lewis pressed against the wall, a leg between his thighs.

Lewis clutched at Bobby's shoulders, his mouth needy as he pushed forward into the first kiss, hunger in every touch and lick. He groaned once, the sound dark and faintly obscene, and Bobby shushed him. "No noise, you can't make a sound."

Lewis bit at his bottom lip and Bobby could see him fighting to do as he'd been told. Bobby opened Lewis' trousers and explored inside.

Warmth and soft skin over hard flesh. Bobby closed his hand around Lewis' cock as he instinctively covered Lewis' mouth with his own, muffling his bitten off cries. Fast and furious, style and finesse sacrificed to speed and the need pulsing through their bodies.

Harsh, dragging tugs and Lewis was gripping Bobby's hips, pulling him closer so he could rut against his body as well as into his hand.

Strangled noises, sounding almost painful, escaped Lewis' mouth. Bobby thrust his tongue deeper, over and over, as Lewis opened wider and just let him.

A few more pulls and it was obvious that Lewis was right there, teetering on the edge, ready to fall. One more and he was gone, spilling into Bobby's grasp, warm and sticky as Bobby cupped his palm ready.

"It's okay, I've got you." Bobby said the words into the soft skin of Lewis' neck.

Lewis panted up at the ceiling, his chest heaving.

But Lewis didn't need the support, he was already moving, his fingers scrambling at the fastenings covering Bobby's groin even as his hand still shook. "You hold still and wait. It's coming." Then he was in, curling around Bobby, his grip tight.

It was Bobby's turn to moan low and resonant, pressing his face deeper into the crook of Lewis' neck as he did so.

"Hang on." Lewis pulled his hand out, ignoring Bobby's sound of protest. "I'll make it better." He spat on his palm a couple of times, then, once more, before wriggling his way back in.

Bobby sighed in pleasure. He could feel his rapid breathing, the thump, thump, thump of his heart in his chest, as Lewis' pulled on him and he fought to stop himself making a sound, compressing his lips tight closed.

"Bite down on my collar." Lewis twisted his head so his lips were in Bobby's hair, as his free hand went to the small of Bobby's back, holding him close. "These scratchy RAF uniforms have to be good for something."

The air hitched in Bobby's chest as he fought back a snort of laughter, but the noise soon turned into a plaintive growl when Lewis upped the pace, ruthlessly taking him to the brink and over. Sinking his teeth into the fabric, Bobby let the feeling roll over him, savoring every sensation as his hips slowed their erratic rocking. He took a few calming breaths and rested his head where it was, Lewis' hand gentle on his back.

Slowly Lewis pulled his hand free, giving Bobby one last squeeze that left him with the sensation for long moments after the grip was gone. Lewis lifted his arm, eyes on Bobby's face as he licked his fingertips clean.

Bobby was powerless to move his gaze from the juncture of tongue and finger.

"I've been trying to imagine what that tasted like all day. Next time, I'll try it direct from the source."

Bobby didn't say a word as he pushed away from Lewis, searching until he found a small towel. He cleaned up before tucking himself away and tidying his clothes, his back to Lewis. Only then did he turn round, stepping close and handing the towel over.

Lewis caught his wrist, dragging him nearer. He tipped his head, a cocky, confident grin smeared across his face, and Bobby almost pulled away. But then the nature of Lewis' smile changed, the self-assurance vanished leaving something softer, more boyish and much gentler. "I kind of feel like I have to ask permission, now all the heat has gone." He ducked his head, eyes lowering to half-mast as he watched Bobby's face. "Can I?" He leaned in, the intention to kiss obvious. But he stopped short, mouths inches apart.

And Bobby understood, understood the hesitancy, the need to ask. If Lewis' smile hadn't changed he wasn't sure if he would have given his consent.

"Sure." The kiss was completely different from the furious taking of moments before. No more biting or thrusting. Now it was a gentle, almost tender exploration. A peaceful fulfilling of other needs as hands skimmed over backs, fingers pressing lightly, testing strength and softness.

No rush but eventually Bobby made a little space between them. "We need to go." His voice was rough, his throat sounding dry. "We need to be seen, seen doing normal things."

"We are 'normal'," Lewis said, louder than Bobby would have liked.

"Come on." He smiled softly. "Sort yourself out and we'll go outside."

* * * *

They sat on the wall in the cool night air, watching as other men made their way back to the sleeping accommodation. Bobby raised a hand in greeting to some as they passed a safe distance away. Lewis lit a cigarette and they shared it in companionable silence for a while. At last Bobby spoke, handing the cigarette back as he exhaled a smoke ring. "You need to be a lot more careful," he said gently, his voice carrying no criticism. "If you'd acted like you did today and you got things wrong, got me wrong, then, well, I think you know the consequences. You'd never get near a Mosquito again, but that would be the least of your problems."

"I..." Lewis' gaze was sharp on Bobby's face. "I was stupid, I went too fast. But it's been a hell of a long time and you... I thought I read you, almost as soon as I saw you."

"That doesn't say a lot for my camouflage skills." Bobby reached for the cigarette, taking a long drag.

"No, I didn't mean... You're not obvious," Lewis said, flustered. "Let's just say I thought I knew, one to another, as it were."

"You did, but what if you were wrong? You were too clear. You didn't leave any room for misunderstanding, even if people didn't want to understand."

"What do you mean, if people didn't want to?"

Bobby sighed, rolling his shoulders back as he ran a hand through his hair. "What we do is illegal and, in the military, what we are is banned. Everyone knows that. But a lot of people also know what goes on and, while they might not condone things, they're willing to turn a blind eye, to pretend they don't know. Only you have to allow them to do that, and if you're so open they can't ignore what's going on..." He let the implication hang in the air.

Lewis took a last drag on the cigarette before stubbing the butt out on the wall beside him. "I didn't mean to compromise you, or myself for that matter."

"You didn't. Everything's fine. I'm concerned about you, though, because if you act like that you'll get caught. You have to be much more discreet and you should never say anything openly."

"Sorry, I—" Lewis took a deep breath, before exhaling slowly through his nose. "I've been a long time without because I haven't thought about sex because my head's been so full of trying to get near the Mosquitoes. They stuck me training nineteen-year-olds to fly Spitfires. How are you meant to show you're worthy of Mossies—as the British call them— doing that? Then I got here and the plane was perfect and you were perfect." He ducked his head, feeling his cheeks burning fiercely, even over the mischievous grin. "I just wanted everything."

"You got everything but trust me, I'm far from perfect."

"Are you concerned about your own position, not just mine?"

"I'd be a fool not to," Bobby admitted.

"But how do you fit in here?"

Bobby picked up the discarded cigarette butt and rolled the squashed mess between his fingers. "I fit in okay. Any perceived quirks I have, the British put down to me being a Yank. They think we're all odd. But I'm sure there are a fair few who know what I am. They deliberately overlook what they might not like because I'm useful—to them, to the war effort." He looked up, staring at Lewis' face. "I work hard at being good at what I do and I want to be useful. I want to fight this war. So I get on with the job and try to fit in and, I think… I hope, people like me well enough. If they don't, they mostly respect me. No one wants to be forced to acknowledge a reason not to."

"Okay." Lewis nodded. "I can do that as well. I'm a good pilot, I can make myself useful. I can fit in. I won't draw attention. But... You and me, please say that wasn't a one-off?"

Bobby regarded him carefully. There were reasons why a man didn't mess with someone he worked with, even more for a man who literally held your life in their hands, but he liked this guy. He seemed open and honest and his enthusiasm was deeply attractive as well as contagious.

"Not a one-off." He couldn't help but lower his head. "Not if you want. It's been a while for me as well."

"Oh, I want, believe me I do." And there was that enthusiasm again.

"But we stay professional and nothing gets taken up in the air."

Once more Lewis nodded. "I'm a little bit desperate and a lot attracted, but not clinically insane." He laughed.

"All right then, we have a plan, of sorts. We just have to be very, very discreet."

"Hey, I just had a thought." Lewis was grinning again. "You're my senior officer, so would you get into trouble for that?"

"That would be the least of my problems." Bobby smiled back. "Unless of course we had sex in the plane—you're the skipper there, regardless of our ranks."

"Now there's an idea." Lewis' eyes grew round in wonder. "In the plane while she's on the ground. Perfect."

"Lewis, I scarcely have room to blink my eyes in the cockpit, you're so huge." Now Bobby couldn't stop laughing. "There's no way we could do anything."

"Give me time." Lewis got up, facing Bobby, his back to the accommodation block. "I'll think of a way."

Bobby had a troubled moment when he wondered if Lewis actually would.

Chapter Two

"Have you heard?" Bobby asked, barely containing his excitement as he threw himself into the seat opposite where Lewis and Dennis were eating breakfast.

"We're actually going to get coffee instead of this awful muck they call tea?" Lewis raised his cup, peering inside with simulated disgust.

Dennis snorted, fork halfway to his mouth. "Nonsense, a good cup of tea is just what you foreign chaps need. It'll make an Englishman of you."

"I don't want to be an Englishm—" But Lewis didn't get any further before he was interrupted.

"Shut up, both of you," Bobby said, exasperated. "This is big time, important stuff." He nodded in acceptance as an orderly put a plate of toast and a large mug of tea in front of him, brushing her away when she asked if he wanted anything else.

"What's going on?" Dennis picked up on his mood.

"I just heard from Roger that a group of four Mosquitoes flew the first operational flight over southern France last week, and word is just being spread. They were only on a reconnaissance mission but they outran German fighters. You know what this means?"

"That the Mosquito is as good as I thought she was." Lewis' eyes shone.

"No, well, yes, but that's not what I meant." Bobby tapped his hand impatiently on the table. "The news means things will soon start—we're going to be taken off testing and actually get authorized as operational. It won't be long before we get to do something useful."

"I... Oh..." was all Lewis could manage, but Bobby scarcely registered his reaction.

"Well, won't that be fun." Dennis raised a hand for the orderly. "I rather think that calls for more tea, don't you?"

* * * *

It was another nine days before word came through that 29 Squadron was both operational and had a mission. Nine days in which Bobby paced endlessly while constantly watching the CO's office, and Lewis could be found reading every technical manual on the Mosquito he could get his hands on.

Nine days when the ground crew almost took the aircraft apart and put her back together, making sure that everything was in perfect working order. On day five Bobby was forced to stand by the plane while Lewis climbed up over the wing and painted a wobbly 'Betty' just under the cockpit window. Then Bobby took over, his neater handwriting and calmer nature making sure that the word was actually legible. Which, he suspected, was exactly what Lewis had wanted all along. By next morning the ground crew had added the outline of a busty woman in a bathing costume and high heels.

They both agreed that neither of their aunts looked anything like her but 'Betty' was staying.

Squadron Leader Roger Harris called them in just before dinner on day nine. He wasn't giving out details, not yet, but he said they were green lit and everyone should get an early night as briefing would be at 0530 hours the following morning.

A gleam came into Bobby's eyes. At last.

Lewis bit at his fingernail and went hunting for coffee.

Bobby found him again much later, sitting on a wooden bench outside the mess hall. He beat out a nervous rhythm with his foot. "I've just spoken to Tilly who says he's given the engine a last once-over and she's running smoother than ever. I'm not sure he trusts us not to damage her. He thinks she's his plane," Bobby said, sitting down beside him.

"I'm sure he's done an excellent job. They all have. We trust them and they should trust us."

"But we get to take her into hostile territory and you know how they complained when you chipped the cowling. That's been fixed and…" Bobby stopped and actually looked at Lewis. "Are you excited? I know I am."

"Of course." Lewis pressed a hand firmly down on his own knee, trying to keep it still.

"But? I can hear it in your voice," Bobby said softly.

"Not sure I should tell you this, not now."

"I think we're long past not telling each other things, don't you? After all, as you said, this is all based on trust."

Lewis sat up, pressing his back into the wooden slats of the bench. He carefully blew out a long breath. "I haven't been on a combat mission before. Tomorrow will be my first."

"But... I thought..." No, Bobby hadn't thought, not really. "How come?"

"All I ever wanted was to fly a Mosquito," Lewis explained, warming to his theme as he went on. "Spitfires and Hurricanes are special but not as special. Turns out I was a good and, most importantly, fast teacher, so after I joined up, they were happy to leave me training new pilots. I didn't want to risk being killed before I got here so I didn't push." He smoothed down the rough material over his knees, hands sure and steady. "I know we're fighting a war, I know this isn't all a big adventure just for me to play with my favorite toy, and I do want to do my part but..." He stopped there, leaving the ending open.

"But you're nervous. That's to be expected."

"Nervous?" Lewis suddenly grinned, wide and infectious. "I'm downright scared."

"Nothing wrong in being scared." Bobby sat back, stretching his legs out in front of him. "Means you've got a brain and you understand the risks. It also means you'll be careful and do things properly. A bombing mission is no place to cut corners in the air, not if you want to do the job right."

"Is that what you think tomorrow will be, a bombing mission?"

"I should think so. Like you keep telling everyone, the Mosquito is too good just to be used for recon. The RAF wants to see what she can do in the field, against real targets. I reckon the mission will be daylight bombing of a fairly important target. That way we can milk the element of surprise for all it's worth, while the Germans don't know about the plane."

"Daylight bombing." Lewis wiped a hand across his mouth, before looking over. "Why aren't you scared?"

"Who says I'm not?" Bobby raised an eyebrow.

"You sure don't look it."

Now it was Bobby's turn to smile. "I might hide the fact well but I'm scared, scared enough that there's some fire in my belly and some adrenaline in my veins. I'm also excited about getting back in the action and actually doing some fighting. It's about time."

"You really want this, don't you?"

"Yes." Bobby nodded. "Yeah, I do. This job is important."

"What were you doing before?" Lewis asked. "I mean before the war and before coming here. I know you joined up a lot earlier than I did."

"I'll tell you, but later." Bobby stood up, looking down. "Not before your—our—first operation together. But trust me, I know what I'm doing and I'll be watching your back the whole time."

"Even though I'm the boss in the air?" It was a weak attempt at humor and Bobby passed right over it.

"Even though you're the skipper, you can depend on me," he said seriously. "Now go to bed and try to get some sleep."

"Okay." Lewis pushed himself to his feet. "We could…" He touched Bobby's sleeve, hand soft but not tentative, not anymore. That wasn't his nature.

"We can do that later as well." Bobby slid his arm gently out from under Lewis' grip, the movement soft, soothing. They'd been managing all right on hand jobs and the occasional blow job. More would be nice, more than nice, but now wasn't the time.

"Promise?"

"Yes, I more than promise, if that's possible. Now sleep, stay scared enough to be sharp and remember, I'll be there all the way."

Lewis held his gaze for a long while as though looking for something. He seemed to find what he wanted, his lips curling in a hint of a smile that warmed his eyes as well.

* * * *

Briefing was at ridiculous o'clock, when they went through every detail of the mission with the pilots and navigators.

Four Mosquitoes were to fly in low and bomb the heavy water factory in Copenhagen, Denmark. Precision bombing. Careful flying. Excellent navigation essential. Important work — this was a mission that could make a big impact on German readiness, that could truly affect the war effort. But one that had to be done right, with accuracy and thoroughness.

Bobby was buzzing at the thought of what was about to happen, knowing at last that he'd be doing something really useful. He came out of the meeting with his head low as he discussed details with the other navigators. These were people he knew reasonably well — as well as you could know anyone in this war — and he'd worked with them before.

Lewis stood to one side, a picture of the outsider. A picture of the nervous outsider just about to mess his pants.

"Come here." Bobby caught him by the shoulder, dragging him toward the group. "You're part of this, a big part."

"I don't know. I'm not seasoned like them and..."

"Shut the fuck up," Bobby said, not angry, more exasperated at the persistent nervousness. That wasn't something anyone normally associated with Lewis. "Don't fall apart, not now." He tried to lace the words with steel, maybe a touch of pretend anger. Anything that would help. Taking a big breath, he tried to say things the way he really meant. "You can't lose it now, not this close. If you do it's not just yourself you're letting down, it's your momma, Texas and the whole reputation of America. The British have been fighting for a long time and they expect a stiff upper lip and all that crap. They let other nationalities in but they never quite expect them to match up. You have to stay strong for all of us."

Still Lewis didn't look convinced.

Bobby took a step back, looking him square in the eye. "You fuck up now and..." He carefully considered the right mix of threat and encouragement. "I'll be disappointed in you."

His words had the effect Bobby was hoping for. Lewis squared his shoulders, straightened his back and drew himself up to his full, impressive height. "What are we standing around here for? We've got a job to do."

Bobby patted him on the shoulder as they strode off toward Betty.

* * * *

Flying in low over the sea, as low as a hundred feet, meant navigation was particularly difficult. The crew couldn't see the enemy coast until they were almost overhead. Then they had to pick up landmarks as quickly as possible. Bobby would be able to identify the railway line he wanted to follow, but it would take him a few moments to determine which direction to go in.

He knew Squadron Leader Harris was leading the operation but he also knew the leader's navigator, Hugo Manning, wasn't as good as he should be. Bobby knew it, Roger Harris knew it — hell, most of the squadron knew it. The only one who appeared not to know was Hugo himself. But Wing Commander Stockton had been at school with Hugo's older brother, which meant that there wasn't a lot anyone could do about him. That was just the way things worked in England.

Everyone also knew Roger relied on Bobby.

Bobby suddenly spotted the silver line of the railway track and relayed the news to the other aircraft with the minimum of fuss.

They flew without incident for a while, enemy planes being caught completely off guard. The calm lasted until they passed a medium-sized industrial town. That was when they encountered their first burst of flak. Bobby watched as Lewis' nostrils flared, his hands tighten on the controls. "If you take her over to the left, the other side of that white tower, and fly a bit higher, we won't be far off the direct route but we'll be out of range."

"I'm not running scared." Lewis looked over briefly.

"I know, but we've got a job to do. We don't want to be shot down before we've dropped our bombs. It's your call, skipper."

Lewis pulled Betty to the left.

Coming in over the outskirts of Copenhagen the flak was heavier and Roger called for them all to take evasive maneuvers. Dennis Banister's plane was caught on the back wing, resulting in a hole that could be clearly seen, even at their distance. He was lucky the wooden structure didn't catch fire.

"Shit," Lewis said, hissing as he craned his head round.

"Steady, skip," Bobby said softly. "He'll be okay, but even if he wasn't you need to concentrate on us. The factory will be coming up soon, which means we'll have to drop to a lower altitude to guarantee accuracy."

Roger Harris went in first, his bombs landing inside the high wall of the factory. The crews of the other aircraft could see the explosions and the cheers rattled through the radios. Dennis went next, taking out the whole front of the main structure. The third Mosquito's bombs looked to finish the job but when the smoke cleared, the back of the building was still intact.

"I guess now's the time for you to prove if you're as good as all the bullshit you've been giving me," Bobby said, goading and smiling like a fool.

"Oh, I'm that good." Lewis grinned, his bravado back at full force now he was totally sure of what he was doing. "I'll bet you a packet of ciggies we hit the target."

"I haven't got any left." Bobby shrugged. "But I'll make it worth your while."

Lewis managed to get them in just right so one bomb went in the hole in the roof Dennis had made. Perfect.

This time there were catcalls as the small group of planes pulled up higher, turning back for home.

Flying over the edge of the city Bobby stretched around to check on all the other aircraft. "Hold on for Roger," he advised. "Hugo's got them off course but Roger will follow us. Now he's got all the glory of leading our first attack, he'll be happy to sit back and enjoy the ride." He was laughing as he talked – the entire base knew how much Bobby, and everyone else, respected their Squadron Leader.

They made it halfway back to the coast before German planes caught them. Six Messerschmitt 109s blocking their way.

Bobby pushed in closer to Lewis, his voice low. "You've proved you're as good as you made out. Now, what about the Mosquito? Are you going to show me just how good your beloved plane really is?"

"You are so on." Lewis' eyes gleamed in anticipation.

Coming out of the sun, light glinting off the propeller blades, engines throbbing with a deep resonance, throttle fully open, they headed for the height of maximum speed. Sitting at Roger's right wing, Lewis pulled the small group to the left then... Then he simply outran the enemy. They whooped with joy as the plane glided through the air, making the very most of all her special qualities.

They pulled into a tight formation, a perfect image of a fighting unit, one to make the breath catch in a man's throat and the pride swell in his chest. As they left the last of the Messerschmitts behind, Roger's voice crackled over the radio, "I think we deserve a bit of a celebration."

All the aircraft followed him in faultless unity as he rose, banking first to the right then the left, before diving over the countryside, pulling out so they flew low enough to almost see the expressions of the onlookers on the ground. Lewis whooped again, the joy plain on his face as the top branches of the trees rustled under the planes' combined power.

Bobby led them back out to sea farther along the coast, away from habitation. Farmland blended into beach then into the smooth, reflective water. Back to base. Home after their first mission. Their first, hopefully successful mission. He knew they had to wait for official confirmation, but everyone was pretty certain they'd done what they'd set out to do and done the job well.

He allowed himself a small smile of satisfaction at the thought, then he worked out the route across the channel.

* * * *

"Man, that was amazing," Lewis said, eyes still gleaming, a buzz in his every movement as he forced his too-large frame through the small hatch of the cockpit. He wriggled, one arm going up above his head as the lapel of his flying jacket caught on the latch, just like it had every other time he'd climbed out.

Bobby unhooked him without saying a word.

Lewis landed, feet on the ground, and pulled off the detested flying helmet, shaking out his hair. "That was just about the most amazing thing in the history of amazing." He couldn't stand still, bouncing from foot to foot as he ran an adoring hand over Betty. "Just amazing."

"Hell, don't tell me, one mission and you're hooked? An adrenaline addict?" Bobby gave a fake groan.

"Forget the mission. Did you see my baby girl?" He was literally petting the plane's wing.

Bobby was sure Lewis would scratch her behind the ears if she had any.

"She was doing three hundred fifty-nine miles an hour and I swear there's more to come. No tail shake and the wing tips stayed true, the engines were downright purring and the controls were light as a feather."

"God, it's even worse." Bobby chuckled as he handed his helmet and radio headgear to one of the ground crew, before collecting his cap and jacket. "You're a Mosquito addict. Let me guess, you're going to bore the pants off us all with technical details?"

"But she's amazing, even better than I thought." Lewis bounced alongside Bobby as they headed for debriefing. "Coming out of that dive she was pulling forces of at least—"

"I don't want to know!" Bobby held up a hand, laughing out loud as he jogged to catch up with the other crews. "You're the pilot and bore—save the lecture for your own kind."

Lewis stopped, grin wide across his face, hands on his hips as he watched. "Damn fool ought to appreciate a thing of beauty and wonder like the Mossie." He looked up then, his gaze catching on the damage to Dennis' plane, where she stood next to theirs. The torn wood and surrounding scorch marks shouted out their message amid the frenetic activity of the ground crew. That had been close, too close. Once more he ran his palm along his plane's fuselage. "Don't worry, darling. I'll take real good care of you."

Senior Aircraftman Tilly, ground crew in charge of Betty's engine, stopped working and watched Lewis. "I understand, sir," he said, his voice full of respect. "After all, she isn't just your baby, and I have a sister called Betty Jean."

* * * *

The Wing Commander was pleased with the results of the raid. Confirmation had come in via local resistance forces on the ground, and the news was all good. The factory would not be operating again in the foreseeable future and only one aircraft had sustained minor damage.

All good.

So good, in fact, that he gave all the crews leave. They didn't have to report back to base until 0800 hours the following morning.

"Right." Dennis rubbed his hands together. "What do you say? I reckon we should all bum a lift into town, hit a pub or two or several. This could be our last night off for a while."

The response was, predictably, enthusiastic. Lewis even stopped complaining about the warm beer by the second pub, singing along badly to songs he barely knew the words to, as Dennis played, equally badly, on the piano. Roger watched from a slightly detached position with a benevolent smile on his face, and Hugo found a new girl in each place.

In the fourth pub of the night Dennis drained the last of his drink, putting the glass down with a loud bang. "Okay, that's my lot. I'm going to say goodbye to you flea-ridden lot and take Daphne dancing. Or maybe to the cinema—there's bound to be a David Niven film on. Perhaps the cinema and dancing."

Roger lifted an eyebrow in a practiced move. "You intend to try dancing after drinking a bathtub of beer? This I have to see. Come on, chaps, Daphne could probably do with a chaperone and Dennis most certainly needs an uninvited audience."

"Leave me alone," Dennis groaned, but the plea was too late — the others were already finishing up.

Outside Hugo made his excuses, arm tight around the latest girl as he slunk away. Bobby took a step back as well. "I'm off too," he said. "Dancing isn't my thing."

There was lots of moaning and half-hearted encouragement but the others knew he wouldn't be budged. Pubs Bobby did, but dancing was a completely different thing.

"Well, I guess I'll have to keep my fellow countryman company." Lewis slapped Bobby on the back of his shoulder. "He's old now. He can't keep up with the rest of us."

"You're not so young." Bobby slapped back. "Not in this war." But they were already waving goodbye to the others and walking along the rain-dampened street.

"So..." Lewis pushed his hands deep into his pockets.

"So?" Bobby copied him.

"The night doesn't have to end now."

"What've you got in mind?"

Lewis pursed his lips, sucking air in nosily. "Thought we might find somewhere a little more private. No one goes near the wooded land at the back of the airfield." He left the idea out there, obviously waiting for a reaction.

"We could." Bobby slowed his step. "Or we could find a room here in town."

Lewis' gaze was on him in a heartbeat, eyes round with surprise and expectation.

"So many servicemen need a temporary place to stay that the place is really crowded and space is hard to come by," he went on. "So crowded we'd almost certainly have to share a room."

"I could live with that." Lewis looked like the sun had come out especially for him. "I could so live with that... I... Now." He grabbed Bobby's sleeve and started pulling him back the way they'd come. "Find somewhere right now."

* * * *

The woman running the boarding house didn't even raise an eyebrow when they asked for a room for the night. Instead she went on about blackout curtains, not dropping ash on her sheets and obeying a hundred other rules. Bobby looked up through his eyelashes, tongue pressed against his bottom lip, and promised to be good.

"And don't you be thinking you can have girls up there," she admonished, already reaching for the key. "I run a respectable house. I'm not having no mucky business."

"Yes, ma'am," Bobby said, in his best Texas drawl.

She slapped the key into his outstretched palm. "You're the last in tonight, you get the attic room. It's only got the one bed and it's cold as a snowman at Christmas, but I don't want to hear no complaints."

Bobby kicked Lewis sharply on the shin to stop his snort of delight.

Much to Bobby's annoyance Lewis practically bundled him up the steep flights of stairs, pushing and poking at him from behind, oblivious of his complaints and attempts to ward off wandering hands. Inside the room, and behind the blessed security of a locked door, it was all needy grappling and desperate kisses. Bobby slid his fingers into

Lewis' hair trying to fix him in place but he couldn't seem to keep still.

"I want... I want..." Lewis tried to say but the sentence went unfinished as he ran his open mouth up the line of Bobby's throat, his teeth catching against stubble.

"What? What do you want?" Bobby eased Lewis back, just enough to see his face.

Lewis exhaled hard, brushing the hair off his forehead. "I want slow and careful, I want detail and time to explore. Hell, I haven't even seen you naked yet."

"We've got all night." Bobby grinned, deliberately slow and dirty.

"Yeah, but I've got so much adrenaline still pumping round my system I'm never going to last."

"So..." Bobby eased off his jacket, hooking it on the back of the chair before slipping his tie through the knot and pulling the material free. "How about we blow each other first and then we can take our time?"

"You genius of a man!" Lewis grabbed him round the back of his neck, pulling him in for a hard, wet kiss. "Knew there was a reason I liked you."

"You mean other than for my wit, charm and innate sense of how to get us to the target and back again while passing as few enemy guns as possible?"

Lewis threw his head back and barked out a laugh. "Yeah, those as well. But right now I want to see you naked. Get moving, boy."

"Boy?" Bobby raised an eyebrow, but he was already unfastening his shirt. "We're back on the ground — that means I'm senior officer, sonny."

"Sonny? You are so on." And Lewis started dragging his clothes off with such speed it was only the thick fabric that prevented the buttons bursting.

The planned consecutive blow jobs turned rapidly into simultaneous ones as desperation proved overwhelming. But that was okay—good, even. It meant the throb in their veins eased enough to let the realization sink in that they really did have time.

They didn't even manage to get all their clothes off for round one—that would have to wait. Shirts were opened or pushed up, trousers thrust out of the way to expose enough flesh to make a man's mouth water. In the few minutes' breathing time before they started again, Bobby lay on his back, gasping for air, hardly aware of the room around him.

"Hey, old man, you can sleep later." Lewis pushed himself onto an elbow, grinning down as he ran a hand up Bobby's chest, undoing the last few buttons as he went.

"First boy and now old man? Make your mind up." Bobby laughed. He felt free, easy and complete. First time he'd felt like that for a long, long time.

"No, it's time for you to make yours up. Either you take your clothes off or I strip you where you lay." Lewis was already trying to pull Bobby's shirt off his shoulders.

"Get off me, you yeti." The thick vein of laughter was still in Bobby's voice. He pushed Lewis' hands away before climbing off the bed. "You'll rip something and then I'd have to think of a reasonable excuse back at base." He slid his shoes under the chair, socks on top. The rest of his uniform he laid out carefully, but his underwear was just thrown in a heap. "You'd leave that to me while you stood there grinning like an idiot and I'd…" He turned round, stopping mid-sentence at Lewis' sharp intake of breath. "What?"

Lewis was already naked, sitting on the bed, propped up against the headboard, staring at him.

"What?" Bobby asked again.

"You..." Lewis' focus was all over him, tracing every line of muscle, every freckle and inch of skin. "You're fucking gorgeous." Lewis sounded awestruck, almost stunned, and still his gaze never left Bobby.

Suddenly Bobby felt more naked than he had in years and he fought the urge to cover his groin with his hands. It was a bit late for that. "Shut up, you shouldn't call a man gorgeous." He climbed on the end of the bed.

"But you are."

"You're not so bad yourself." He crawled up Lewis' body, deliberately slowly.

"But you're gorgeous and..." The enthralled quality faded from Lewis' voice, replaced by pure lust. "I get to play with all this." He ran his hands down Bobby's sides, resting them on his hips.

"We get to play." Bobby kissed him, slow and gentle, taking his time now that he didn't have to be furtive. "We get to take our time and play all night."

Time. Time to map Lewis' skin with his fingers and mouth, to explore and experiment, finding ways to elicit a breathy sigh, a bitten off moan. To test softness and strength, to taste and smell and touch without fear of discovery or the ever-present need for speed.

Most of all, the time to kiss when need was gone. To enjoy the simple pleasure for its own sake, without thoughts of the act leading elsewhere, of it being for any other purpose.

Bobby dug his fingers deep into Lewis' hair, twisting and pulling to get just the right angle, the perfect position, licking over lips and deep inside until both their mouths were puffy and wet.

"God, I like this." Lewis lifted himself up on one arm, just enough to speak. "Taking my time, having you naked. It's all good."

"It can get better." Bobby pushed himself back into the pillows, raising one knee up and letting it fall open, laughing as Lewis' eyes widened.

"Really? I get to go first?"

"Told you I'd make it worth your while." He pulled up the other leg.

Lewis was already scrabbling around for something slick. "If all senior officers motivated their men like you do this war would be over by Christmas."

"If they all did it like I do half the forces would be on their knees."

Lewis stopped, a small bottle held in his hand. "On my knees? Later, I've got something else to do first."

"I meant with exhaustion but, hell, I like the way you think."

It wasn't the only thing Bobby liked.

He liked what came next, loved it. Loved every moment as he was pushed up the bed with each intoxicating thrust. He braced himself with one hand above his head, against the headboard, the other clutched at Lewis' shoulder as he let himself roll in the pleasure, letting the feeling consume him and bring him slowly to a peak.

Slow and thorough, deep and hard enough so he'd feel the results for a while. Just the way he liked it. Just what he wanted.

Afterward he thought he could really do with the clichéd cigarette but he knew he'd given his last to Hugo. "We got anything to drink?" he asked Lewis instead.

"Only tap water." Lewis laughed out loud suddenly, and Bobby realized what an everyday occurrence it was with him. An everyday occurrence to laugh wholeheartedly and freely like that. Everyday and very welcome. "I got a little over-excited when you suggested coming here and didn't plan ahead." He got up, and filling a glass with water from the cracked sink in the corner, he handed it to Bobby then rooted around in the pocket of his discarded jacket for a handkerchief, wetting the cloth before cautiously cleaning himself up. "Fuck that's goddamned cold but nothing came out the hot tap when I tried it."

"Someone else has used all the hot water." Bobby held out his hand for the handkerchief. "This is England, wartime, they run out all the time. You'll get used to it."

Lewis got back into bed, shivering dramatically, and pulled the covers over them as Bobby discarded the handkerchief on the floor. He pressed in close, touching from shoulder to knee, and hooked his ankle over Bobby's. "Can I ask you something?"

"Sure. I'm not guaranteeing I'll answer, though. You don't need to know where I keep my stash of authentic bourbon."

"You've got bourbon? You shouldn't have told me because I'll find it," Lewis said confidently. "But that wasn't my question."

"So?"

"Why are you here?" He tipped his head so he could see Bobby's face. "I mean why are you in the RAF?"

"I came here because..." Bobby twisted, not pulling away but sitting up against the headboard. He linked his hands behind his head and stretched his elbows back, thinking carefully before he spoke. "Because I don't think this war is anything like the last one. I think this time the fight is against something truly evil, something that has to be stopped. I believe in this war."

"So you wanted to fight?"

"Yes. I came over to Europe in the middle of the Spanish Civil War, stayed there until the fighting ended, then moved to England. You could feel war coming—there was something in the air, something big. I wanted to be part of it."

"Why? Because of politics?"

"Mostly." Bobby exhaled slowly. "Freedom, democracy, standing up against fascism. They're important ideals, ones worth fighting for and building a life around. I want to fight for what I believe to be right."

"You're here because you believe in the fight." Lewis looked down at where his hands rested on the covers, before going on. "Not just because you wanted to play with the planes."

"I'm fighting for a cause, but that doesn't make my effort any more valuable than yours." Bobby placed his hand over Lewis'.

"I was so scared today. Terrified when we met the flak," Lewis admitted. "When I saw Dennis had been hit, suddenly everything stopped being a game and became real. I... I wanted to run away. Run or fly away."

"But you didn't and that takes guts."

"Even if I'm not fighting for the cause in the same way?" Lewis met Bobby's gaze again.

"Why are you fighting?"

"Because..." Lewis ran a hand up through his hair, making the strands stand up at odd angles. "Because even I could see Hitler needed to be stopped. Because

I thought England needed all the help she could get." He shrugged. "Something like that."

"Those are good reasons, and they show you aren't here just for the Mosquito."

"But the plane is a big part of it. I knew the Mossie could make a real difference and I wanted to be involved."

"You wanted to make a difference. That sounds like fighting for something you believe in to me," Bobby assured him.

"Maybe." Lewis nodded. "Whatever the reason, I'm going to make a difference now I'm here. What about you? Are you hiding out in a Mosquito squadron because of what you, we, are?"

Again Bobby stopped and thought for a moment. A man didn't have conversations like this often and this one felt important. It mattered that he said things right. "I'm queer. I've known it for a long time. But that's not who I am, not what makes me *me*. There are other things that are more important to me than who I sleep with," he said with conviction. "Is it that important to you?"

"Being queer?" Lewis screwed his face up in an odd way as he gave the question serious thought. "Yeah, it's important to me. I'm not going to try to change, even if it is especially difficult with the war."

"I'm not going to change either but I guess sex isn't that significant to me." Bobby suddenly grinned infectiously "Now you know why I hadn't had any for a good while. I hadn't found anyone who got me interested."

"Until you met me." Lewis smiled back.

Bobby tipped his head in acknowledgment. "Until I met you."

"Now you've admitted one of your secrets, tell me the rest," Lewis pressed. "You're older than most of the guys around, especially at your rank. If you've been in Spain, been here since the start of the war, why are you flying ops in a fairly new plane?"

Bobby sat and stared at Lewis, deciding how much he wanted to share. "They tried to get me behind a desk, a fairly important one, but…" It was his turn to shrug. "I want to actually be out there fighting, not stuck back where it's safe, telling others to take the risks. I trained as a bombardier first, then thought about becoming a pilot but I don't have the touch." He pulled himself farther up until he was square against the headboard and he could turn his whole body toward Lewis. "You think Mosquitoes are going to make a huge difference – well, I think the same about good navigation. Think about it – with a first class navigator we'll be able to go deep into enemy territory, pinpoint the target, then do real damage without wasting bombs. Imagine what a difference that would make."

"Yeah." Lewis dragged himself up as well, eyes unfocused as though he were trying to visualize the scenario. "But for that to work without massive losses you'd need a damn good plane and a pilot who could really fly." He looked over to Bobby, who was staring hard at him.

"You keep telling me the Mosquito's a damn good plane and I know you can really fly," Bobby said.

"You, me and Betty. We're your perfect combination, your fantasy team." Lewis could feel it, feel Bobby's dream of the ultimate fighting, bombing unit. Bobby could see realization clear on his face.

"We're the perfect team. We're going to make a difference."

Chapter Three

Early December 1941

Seven operations in short succession and the whole squadron was feeling the strain as well as getting into the stride of how things worked. Early morning briefing, a hearty breakfast of whatever was available, check the aircraft over thoroughly, a last nod to the other crews and the ground staff, then away. They were going deeper into enemy territory, pushing the limits and the speed of the planes, testing the accuracy of their bombing.

And they were getting better. Their precision bombing was as good as, if not better than, anything that had been seen before. Bridges, buildings, factories, railway junctions, even munitions dumps. They all came under attack, all were destroyed.

But there was bound to be a cost.

The first time they came back with the belly of the plane scorched black and dented, the wheel mechanism creaking and groaning, shudders of protest running through the whole structure as they came down, Bobby's mouth had gone dry and his belly had tightened. He'd seen aircraft land without wheels, seen them skid across the airfield. Seen them flop and come to a halt if they were lucky. Seen them crash and burst into flames if they weren't.

Lewis had to forcibly kick open the cockpit hatch as Tilly pulled from the other side, angling to bypass the damage as he pushed himself out. He ran his hands over the damaged surface then, his face drawn. "Sorry, baby girl," he whispered. "I'll do better next time."

Tilly didn't say a word at the sight of Lewis' face.

Next time they'd brought Betty back without a scratch on her.

The time after she was clear but Lewis was holding himself tight as Bobby watched him march away, only to throw up at the side of the control tower. Two Mosquitoes had been shot down that day. Two crews were dead. It was the first time that Lewis had lost anyone he knew well. Bobby gave him room and pretended not to notice.

After dinner all the crews went to the local pub, as if in an unacknowledged tribute to those who had been lost. Warm beer was drunk, everyone talked long and loud, but the missing faces were keenly felt.

That evening, alone in Bobby's room, Lewis had pressed him back against the wall, hands splayed on his hips, mouth fast and deep on Bobby's cock. And if he pressed too hard, gripped too tight, arched his fingers so they dug in too far, too intensely? Well, Bobby figured he couldn't blame him. He also ignored the bitten back noises that sounded too much like sobs, letting them both have the pretense of pleasure cries.

Bobby ignored the whispered words, "Don't die, I won't let you. I'll keep you and Betty safe," as Lewis pressed his face against Bobby's hip, his mouth open, his breath warm and damp.

* * * *

Bobby looked up from his forced inspection of Betty's engine as a Jeep pulled up next to them. They were supposed to be finding out about a new modification Tilly had made, and Lewis was very excited about it. But Bobby had lost track of the discussion at least ten minutes ago. That was if he'd ever understood it.

"The CO wants to see you two in the control room immediately," Dennis said, as he pushed open the car's door. "The situation is serious, very serious. The bloody Japanese have just bombed your chaps at Pearl Harbor."

Bombed Pearl Harbor?

If the Japanese had bombed the US Naval Base at Pearl Harbor, Hawaii, that meant... Bobby started to work out the implications as soon as the initial shock wore off. America would have to retaliate, they'd have to declare war, and not just in the Pacific — against the Japanese.

America was going to war.

He glanced over at Lewis, who appeared to be having even more trouble taking everything in. "Come on." He tugged at Lewis' shoulder. "Let's get over there and find out what's happening."

The control room had a hushed atmosphere as everyone worked almost silently, listening to the RAF radio that brought the latest news. It was a massive attack with hundreds of aircraft hitting the base and the ships in it. The estimate of casualties was vague but into four figures.

Lewis and Bobby were ushered in then left to listen as more detail came through. Lewis perched on a high stool, his elbows on his knees, his chin resting on his clasped hands as he stared into the middle distance and concentrated on what he heard. Bobby leaned back against the wall behind him.

A couple of hours later it was Roger who called them out. "If anything else significant happens someone will find you and let you know. But you need to press on now—we have work to do and I think it's more important than ever. I've got the mess to save you some dinner. Go, eat, and then get some sleep. We'll be flying tomorrow. Our war isn't over just because fighting has started up somewhere else as well."

Bobby knew he was right. If anything, what was happening at Pearl Harbor made winning this part of the war more important than ever.

They ate in silence for a while as Lewis pushed around his gray, over-cooked vegetables and watery mashed potato before giving up and putting his fork down. "What do we do now?" he asked.

"Today? Tomorrow? We carry on as normal. After that?" Bobby shrugged. "I'm not sure."

"They will declare war, won't they?"

"I don't see how they can do anything else. Not now. I don't see how anyone can argue for isolationism after an attack like that."

"And when they do declare?" Lewis' eyes fixed on Bobby's. "What do we do?"

"I don't know." Bobby thought things through as he spoke. "There's going to be a lot of American guys in the RAF who will want to join the US Army Air Force immediately. But I don't know how it would work. The Eagle Squadrons are entirely American so they can't all just leave at the same time. That doesn't seem right and I'm not sure they'd all want to go."

"What about us? Do we go?"

"You want me to make the decision for both of us? That's not how it should be."

Lewis licked over his lips, gaze never leaving Bobby's face. "I want to know what you think. What you think we – or just you – should do."

"And then you'll make your own decision?"

"And then I'll tell you what I think."

Bobby regarded him for a long, long moment. "All right." He sat back in his chair, ignoring the empty room around him. "I want to stay here. The RAF let me join, trained me, trusted me and my skills – I don't want to let them down."

"So you want to stay out of loyalty?"

"Partly." Bobby acknowledged. "But also because here we're fighting Germany, fascism. This is a war I feel fervently about and…" He pushed his empty plate away as though it were something more, something connected to the events of the day. "These people have been fighting for two years already. I was allowed to join in and I admire them, owe them, but they're also organized. It'll take the US time to get going and the British are fighting now. I want to stay."

"Then we'll stay," Lewis said with quiet certainty.

"We? I can't make that decision for you."

"You haven't." Lewis tipped his head in agreement. "I wanted to be here because of Mosquitoes and I'll stay because of them, because of you. Hell, Bobby, we're a team. It's you, me and Betty."

"People are dying every day," Bobby said. "Teams are split all the time."

"Yes, but together the three of us are damn good, better than we are separately. You know it, I know it and the commanding officers know it. I figure they'll keep us together for as long as they can." His voice dropped, every bit as serious as Bobby. "You wanted to make a difference — well, so do I, and I think together we'll make a hell of a difference right where we are. If that means I get to stay with the Mosquitoes, well, that's a bonus I'd never turn down."

"Okay." Bobby nodded. "If you're sure then we'll both stay. Now I guess Roger was right — we need to sleep so we're ready for tomorrow."

When they returned to base after the next day's operation it was to the news that the United States had declared war.

* * * *

Two days later nine Mosquitoes were sent to destroy mines in Norway. It should have been a simple mission. First Hugo almost got them all lost on the way out. Bobby snapped his annoyance to Lewis, noticing the deviation from the intended path before anyone else. But it was difficult to criticize over an open radio system like the one they used. Fifteen minutes later the air in the cockpit had gone blue and Lewis had had enough.

"Fucking say something," he said, to Bobby, after first switching off his mic.

"You fucking say something, you're the skipper."

"I'm a Pilot Officer and he's related to the Queen or something."

"He's not royal, you asshole."

"Maybe, but he is two ranks higher than me. You tell him."

"He's a rank higher than me, and you're a pilot while he's only a navigator."

"Only a navigator?"

Bobby could practically hear the raised eyebrow in Lewis' voice. "You know what I mean. If we don't do something soon we'll be bombing Canada."

Lewis sucked in a huge breath, before letting the air out slowly. "Okay." He switched his mic back on. "Roger," he called to the Squadron Leader. "I have a problem. I know we're probably taking a more...elaborate route to avoid enemy aircraft or guns, but I'm not sure I'll have enough fuel to get home if we go too much farther off the planned course."

There was a long moment of silence from all the aircraft before Roger's voice came over the air. "Situation acknowledged. Get your navigator to plot us the quickest way to the target."

"Thank you," Bobby mumbled, head bent low over his maps. "Although I bet Hugo will still be annoyed at me when we get back."

"It's not your fault you're better than him, and you're welcome. I bet he'll be annoyed with me as well."

When they reached the target they realized it should have been easy to hit but it wasn't. The Germans had deliberately attempted to camouflage the specific buildings they were aiming for if they were to disrupt production as much, and for as long, as intended. The only way to identify the right target was to fly in low. "But that means the planes behind could be blinded, or even hit, by the blast from the bombs dropped by the plane in front," Bobby said anxiously.

"What else can we do? What other option is there?" Lewis asked.

Roger took the decision out of their hands by ordering that they come in with a much longer gap than normal. A long enough gap for anti-aircraft guns to be trained on them. Lewis blew out a long breath and did as he was told.

They lost one plane but hit and destroyed the target.

On the way home they met incoming enemy aircraft right at the moment they thought they were clear. Keeping in tight echelon they rose up to a higher altitude and managed to outrun them, but everyone was exhausted by the time they made it back to base.

That night the tension was palpable in the mess around Hugo, and Lewis and Bobby stood as far away as possible. But any discomfort was eased by the numerous drinks bought for them by other crews.

Next day Bobby turned a corner and accidentally bumped into Hugo and Roger, heads close together as they talked seriously. They turned their backs when they saw him and Hugo was in a quiet, thoughtful mood afterward.

That evening he bought everyone a drink.

Being exhausted didn't mean they got to rest, though. Next day they went after a diesel plant. Eight Mosquitoes left the airfield and eight made it back but Roger's plane had two holes in its starboard engine cover. He'd been caught by flak while waiting for the aircraft in front to drop their loads. Lewis' face blanched and Bobby had squeezed his knee, keeping his hand there for longer than he should have. Roger was the leader, the boss. Everyone trusted and valued him. The thought of losing him... Yeah, Bobby felt that.

Later, in the mess, they argued about ways of getting round the situation. Eventually someone came up with the idea of delayed fuses. The discussion got intense as they went through options and practicalities. On the next operation – a weapons supply depot for which they had to come in at low level once more – some bombs went off after ten minutes, some an hour. The last didn't explode for a few hours, when the Germans were trying to salvage the plant.

As Dennis had pointed out, they would all be drinking back at base when the bombs exploded.

They carried on working, the squadron at full alert, right up to Christmas and through the holiday period. New Year's Eve saw the squadron limping back from a raid deep into France. They'd hit a huge storm long before they could see the Channel and Lewis and Bobby had shrunk down into the cockpit as the thunder and lightning crashed what felt like feet away.

"Jesus, fucking shit," Lewis groaned between clenched teeth.

"It'll be fine," Bobby said, although he wasn't sure if he was reassuring Lewis or himself.

They'd both sighed in relief as they had counted the latest roll of thunder, which had to be over a mile away. Somehow, though – in what Bobby thought was a typical show of bloody English irony – the next flash of lightning hit them.

"Fuck," Lewis said again, looking out of the window. "There's a ball of fire just sitting on the wing and laughing at us."

Bobby held his breath but inexplicably the flames suddenly died out.

When they got back to the airfield there wasn't a mark on the plane and Bobby couldn't quite believe their luck.

* * * *

On New Year's Day they both rang their families, even though transatlantic calls weren't easy or cheap. Lewis had told Bobby that his mother would gather as many of the family together around the telephone at the agreed time as she could, and he was right. He moaned that he could barely make out any individual voice, or who was wishing him Happy New Year. It didn't matter, though — he heard them and they heard him. The rest of the mess hall heard them all shouting and laughing. It was better than a letter.

Bobby went after him, still smiling at the noise from Lewis' family. His phone call was quieter but equally welcome.

Later they sat in old deckchairs, muffled up against the cold, and watched as the ground crew worked on the plane. "It's strange," Lewis said, wrapping his hands around a hot mug of tea. Bobby had predicted that Lewis would get used to it and he was right. There wasn't much choice because, in the RAF, you simply had to drink tea and he'd almost admitted he liked it. "America is in the war now but I guess things won't have changed there much. No one is bombing them, there isn't rationing like here, nor the immediate sense of danger."

"I like things like this," Bobby admitted. "I want to fight but I like knowing my mom is safe back there. It makes me feel..." He shrugged. "I don't know, better about things."

"Like there's somewhere to go home to?"

"Maybe." But Bobby didn't sound confident.

"You don't intend to go back?" Lewis swung round to stare at him.

Again there was a shrug—one Bobby knew was intended to look casual but just missed the mark. "I'm not sure I'd fit, not someone like me."

"You mean...?" Lewis gave a brief gesture to include them both.

"Hell, yeah. My mom would still welcome me but my political views were bad enough for those outside the family. They didn't exactly win me any friends. And if I got caught doing what we do in my part of Texas I'd probably be lynched."

Lewis was silent for a moment. "Remember, I come from Texas as well," he said at last.

"How did you manage?"

Lewis gave a snort of humorless laughter. "By not having sex within a couple of hundred miles of the state."

"That's a hell of a way to live."

"Tell me about it. There has to be something better, somewhere in the world."

"Maybe there is but, I reckon, before we start thinking about that we have a war to win."

"The war comes before the personal freedom and happiness of men like us?"

"Lewis." Bobby pulled himself up in his chair. "This war comes before anything else."

* * * *

On the 9th of January the squadron was given five days' leave. Most of the men whooped with joy because that was enough time to get home and see their families. Lewis and Bobby looked at each other ruefully, knowing they didn't have a hope in hell of seeing theirs.

"We could go to London," Bobby suggested indifferently. "It's being bombed but I heard there's a real party atmosphere. Everyone wants to have a good time before their head gets blown off."

"I've had enough of bombs for a while. I want somewhere quieter for a few days. Anyone got any ideas?" Lewis asked the room at large.

"You could try the seaside," someone suggested. "It's a bit grim in January but you might be able to buy an ice cream and walk along the seafront."

"Wow, that sounds like fun." Bobby pulled a face.

"You can't even do that," one of the other navigators said. "They've put defenses along the beach to stop landings, so you'll get caught in the barbed wire or shot by the Home Guard."

"Great. Then I guess it'll have to be London," Lewis said, slouching in his chair and acting like an eight-year-old told to do his homework. His pout would have been funny if it hadn't been so earnest.

"Can you fish?" Hugo lifted his head up from where he was engrossed in his newspaper.

They looked at each other. "I suppose so. I went once, when I was a kid. It can't be that hard to remember, can it?" Bobby shrugged at the others questioningly.

"If you'd like, you're welcome to use the family's cottage in Surrey," Hugo went on. "The place is a good mile walk from the nearest town and there's nothing to do except bloody fish, but there're no bombs and it's warm and comfortable."

"Are you sure?" Bobby didn't know what to make of the offer. "That's very kind of you."

"It's the least a chap can do." Hugo brushed the compliment away. "You scratch my back and all that sort of thing."

Lewis and Bobby stared at each other a little confused but seriously considering the offer.

"Do you want to spend five days stuck with just me?" Bobby asked.

Lewis caught Bobby's gaze for a moment, his eyes intent, then he dropped his head, the angle and his hair shielding his eyes from everyone in the room. "Yes," he murmured.

They caught the train the following morning.

* * * *

The cottage was indeed over a mile's walk, along lanes with no paths and in the pouring rain. Bobby turned up the collar of his heavy coat but the action made no difference as the cold water still found its way inside. Lewis had refused to be put off, saying that late trains, the lack of road signs and locals who glared at them as if they were Nazi executioners, rather than servicemen in their own Air Force, would not dampen his cheerful mood.

Bobby listened as Lewis explained for the tenth time that getting time off, time off alone together, made him happy, and he was going to enjoy it.

Inside, the cottage was warm and welcoming. The 'lady who does' had visited that morning, pulling wide the yellow checked curtains, opening a window to air the place, lighting the fire and leaving basic food supplies. There was even a small cracked vase on the table with a few rather bedraggled winter pansies. The cottage wasn't the chic, stylish place they had expected of Hugo's family. Instead, the small rooms had a lived-in air that made it feel much more comfortable.

Bobby watched as Lewis looked around and his eyes gleamed even before he started exploring. He laughed aloud at Lewis' excited expression when he realized there was just one bedroom with one large bed. There was a fireplace in the corner, a basket of logs next to it, and a huge, thick patchwork quilt on the side.

Lewis declared the cottage perfect and Bobby couldn't disagree. It was just what they needed. A place to relax, to sleep, to recover and spend some real time alone together.

They spent the first day in bed. A soft and gentle day when they took their time to enjoy the luxury of all the hours with nothing to do and the freedom to make as much noise as they, as Lewis, wanted. After their own private, delayed Christmas dinner, Bobby took Lewis back to bed and spent the afternoon lazily exploring all that skin. Finally, when Lewis was almost incoherent with the need to come, he fucked him slow and methodically.

Time. Time was the big luxury they'd never had and Bobby was going to savor every second.

Time to lose himself and luxuriate in Lewis' body. Forgetting himself and everything that was going on. Principles? The need to fight? Death and destruction? All lost in sweat and slick, cocks and fucking. Enjoying sex was different when he knew the man so well. That was something new, something Bobby had never experienced before. Not just enjoying skin, but also the man inside. He loved the physical, the feeling of stretching and being stretched, the play of hard muscle under his fingertips, of tight flesh between his teeth, of long limbs wrapped around him. Knowing he liked the man inside the body took everything to another level.

Pushing Lewis' hair back behind his ears as he smiled or watching his face as he slept, seeming so young, so innocent, with smooth skin across sharp bones. So different from the face he wore when flying, bombing.

Enjoying Lewis' cries, the way his face slackened as he came, the way he grabbed at Bobby. Even allowing himself to enjoy the way Lewis pulled him close and held him tight afterward.

Lewis had wanted to talk then, after the sex, but Bobby wouldn't, couldn't. He wasn't ready.

That didn't come until the next morning when they were bundled up in their thick flying jackets, sitting attempting to fish by the lake that, secretly, Bobby thought was devoid of life. Even then it needed Lewis to start the conversation, with his stumbled attempts to discuss their 'relationship'.

A word Bobby hated with a passion.

He took pity on Lewis, trying to make things easy for him. "Hey, it's okay," he reassured, as Lewis stumbled over his latest explanation of what it meant to be a gay man in the forces, of what they were together. "I know what queer men are like, especially now with the war. Everyone is fucking everyone else and I understand why. The straight folks are doing it as well. Anybody could be killed at any time, so we live for the moment, take all we can get. It makes sense and why not? I understand."

Lewis suddenly sat up, ignoring his fishing rod as he stared at Bobby. "But you don't want that, do you?"

"I…" Bobby faltered over the words. "I don't know. Maybe not."

"You want more?"

He looked at him, but only for a moment before his attention went back to his float, bobbing on the water.

"I have a little more, here, now, with you. But don't worry — things don't have to be heavy. It's okay like that because, let's face it, it's probably for the best. This war isn't going to end any time soon."

"But you want more." This time it wasn't said as a question. It sounded like Lewis was just stating what he knew. "You want long term."

"I…" Again Bobby ground to a halt. That wasn't what he intended to say. 'More' wasn't something a man could think about, not when he was queer. And that was before there was a war.

"You do." Lewis' voice sounded warm, a smile thick in the words.

"Long term, if there is a long term anymore? Ideally? Yeah, maybe I would like that." Bobby ran a hand through his hair. It wasn't fair to put pressure on someone like this, that wasn't right. But he'd vowed to himself to be honest and, for him, that meant staying quiet or telling the truth, even if, maybe, he didn't want to. "I could so easily fall in love with you. I…" His voice dropped to a whisper. "I think I'm halfway there already. But it's all right, there's no pressure, I'm happy with what we have. I'm not a fool."

"Halfway?" Lewis twisted to face him, his expression as open as always. "I hope you're more than that, because I'm already full way in love with you and it'd be a damn shame if you didn't love me back."

Bobby stared over, surprised, his whole body registering the shock. "Really?"

"Don't look so stunned, it makes you look like a fish out of water." Lewis reached out and patted Bobby's knee quickly, the gesture friendly but also so much more. "I love you." He shrugged as though it should have been a difficult statement to make when it honestly wasn't. "I love your honesty, your commitment, your passion and your politics. All right." He shrugged again. "Maybe I don't always understand your politics, but you believe in them and I believe in you."

"You believe in me?" Bobby couldn't quite take everything in. Things like this didn't happen in his world, or in any world he knew, especially not to him.

"Of course I do. I trust you, I believe in you." Lewis carefully and very deliberately laid his palm flat on Bobby's thigh. "I love you and I want this. You, me, us. Now calm down and accept the situation."

"I am calm." Bobby couldn't stop the snap in his voice. He was way off balance and he knew it. "I just... I... This sort of thing isn't common, not for our sort."

"Only heterosexuals can fall in love?" Lewis pulled a face full of disdain. "Now you're being stupid and downright insulting."

"And you're being an idiot," Bobby shot back. This whole conversation was getting away from him, when he'd been so sure of what he wanted to say. He'd wanted to reassure Lewis that there was no pressure, that things could stay easy between them. Instead Lewis had knocked him sideways. "Stop acting like it's all so easy — nothing's easy when you're queer."

Lewis stared at him, seeming almost weary of the fight. "You're right, it's not easy and I'm trying to make things sound that way. But, to me, they are. Either or both of us could be dead tomorrow so why worry about the future? You said everyone is living for today, so fine, we'll do that, because today I love you and it really is that easy."

"But..." Bobby got up, dropping his rod and stalking to the edge of the bank, his hands thrust deep into his pockets. He stared out over the water for a long while, his chest rising and falling, before he turned round. He hadn't expected this, wasn't ready for the way he'd been knocked off keel. He'd made a fundamental mistake and underestimated Lewis.

He wouldn't make that mistake again.

Be honest. "I guess I've always hoped for something more but I never even allowed for the possibility of it actually happening. That was just a daydream."

Lewis didn't move from his seat, stretching his neck back to look up at him. "We mean something, Bobby, and I want that. I know this scares you, us, queer, in a world that doesn't understand or approve. But you have it, it's real, so let yourself believe and enjoy what we have."

"I'm not sure I know how."

"Then that's my job. To make sure we both get what we need, what we deserve."

Bobby pressed his lips tight together, holding his breath. Then he gave one short, sharp nod as he caught hold of his chair and dragged it close to Lewis' before finding his rod and sitting down so their knees brushed together.

Lewis patted the back of his neck then left his hand there.

Chapter Four

End of February 1942

By now, 29 Squadron had been moved and moved a second time. They'd gone from one end of England to the other and, for a couple of weeks, to Scotland. Lewis had enjoyed their time that far north, enjoyed flying ridiculously low over empty landscapes, into and out of valleys in practice for various operations, but the continuous rain had ended up getting Bobby down. Even Dennis said his feet were always damp, even inside his plane.

After a difficult two weeks, when they'd flown missions almost every day, the whole squadron was sent for practice on the new fighter version of the Mosquito. Bobby loved the guns and the immediate sense of power they gave. Lewis admitted the plane was "cool" and "all right, in its own way" but insisted it wasn't a patch on Betty.

The fighter couldn't carry the bomb load Betty could, so Bobby had to admit he was sort of right. The fact didn't matter anyway because, after another evening spent with everyone arguing the merits of fighters and bombers, the squadron was sent back to their bombers.

Lewis thought the whole thing was madness, a waste of time and training. Bobby defended Command, saying they just wanted them ready for anything, although he secretly suspected it had just been a mighty cock-up.

They ended up back at the airfield they'd started at, much to everyone's delight, including Lewis. He'd insisted that they revisit the boarding house at which they'd spent their first night together. Bobby thought it was a silly, sentimental idea but he was proved wrong. The night was sweaty, dirty and perfect, and left him feeling the burn for days after.

Their stay didn't last long. Twelve days and the loss of two planes later, they moved again. This time to an airfield in southern Kent, closer to the coast, where they settled.

It was only a few days after they had settled in when Hugo was killed in action. His plane was shot down on the French side of the channel, by guns stationed on the ground, caught in the wrong place at the wrong time.

For once, the situation hadn't been his fault.

He was simply unlucky. German fighters had singled out his plane, pushing it away from the rest of the formation and into the path of the guns. The rest of the squadron had watched as the incident had happened, as his plane had been hit and had gone down in a ball of flames. There could have been no survivors.

Bobby took it all in, said his own silent prayer then added another, thanking every deity he could think of that Roger had caught chicken pox from his youngest son and was currently in bed, back at base.

As they flew home over the calm waters, searching for the first signs of the white cliffs at Dover, Lewis reached out, clasping the back of Bobby's neck. The grip became painful, his fingers pushing up under the flying helmet to tighten in his short hair. Bobby didn't say a word. Instead, he angled his head closer, pushing into the hold.

That night they were back in another little attic room in another local town. The landlady was just like the previous one, saying the same speech every time. There was no room, they were late, they'd have to share the room right at the top. It didn't matter if they arrived at midnight or right after dinner, if there were already lots of service personnel staying or only a couple—she always said the same thing.

She knew, they knew she knew, she knew that. This was a game played out everywhere to protect everyone.

The sex was fast, furious and just the right side of painful. They both held on too tight, pressed too hard, fucked too deep, ignoring anything but their own needs, even as the other groaned. The groans weren't of pain, not really, but even if they were, they were barely noticed in the avalanche of feelings that left them reeling.

As Lewis thrust in hard, with Bobby's knee bent up in ways it didn't want to go, his fingernails left long tracks of scraped flesh across Bobby's freckles.

Bobby bit down much too hard on Lewis' shoulder. Teeth marks under love bites with a hint of blood that would be there for days and days. As long as the bruises on his own hips.

Eventually Bobby propped himself up on his side, with an elbow on the bed, stroking his other hand down Lewis' neck and out over the damaged skin. There were spider's webs of broken veins radiating from the bite marks. "Sorry," he said, but even he could hear that it didn't sound completely sincere.

"Sorry as well." Lewis briefly touched the bruises on Bobby's hip, the bites on his inner thigh.

"Doesn't matter." Bobby shook his head.

"As long as I didn't hurt you." Lewis slid his hand back over the curve of Bobby's side to the rounded flesh of his buttocks, the very tips of his fingers just ghosting over the crease.

"You didn't." They both knew it was a lie but they also knew any pain wouldn't last long. "Isn't important anyway."

"I..." Lewis sucked in a huge breath, and Bobby could see him push down all the emotions in his chest. They were still there, but no one had any idea how to deal with them. "I was so scared."

"Nothing wrong with being scared." Bobby traced over the marks on Lewis' shoulder, following their pattern.

"You'd think I'd be used to the feeling by now—enough people have already died. But this was different, this was..." He looked up at Bobby, his eyes huge and round. "And even now things could be worse. Not that Hugo wasn't important, that I don't care, because I do. It's just that, hell, what if it had been Dennis or Roger?"

"It could be either of them any day, you know that," Bobby said very softly, his hand never leaving or stilling on Lewis' skin.

"What..." Lewis' voice seemed to fail him, his very breath, as a shudder ran through his body. "What if it had been you?"

"It won't be me." He leaned forward and very, very gently kissed the marks he'd left earlier.

"You can't say that, can't know that." Lewis protested.

"Yes, I can." Bobby met his gaze, holding it steady.

"How?"

"Because we're a lucky pairing."

"What?" Lewis pushed and Bobby ended up flat on his back. He slipped his hand over Lewis' shoulder as Lewis loomed above him.

"I have this theory," Bobby said calmly. "There's a very rare phenomenon, but I swear I've seen it before. There are lucky pairings and we're one of them. If we stick together we'll be okay, trust me."

"That's nuts." Lewis shook his head.

"But true. We're both going to get through this. We're lucky."

"I... You... But— You're insane."

"But right." Bobby smiled, warmly. "We're lucky."

"You..." Lewis gave a gust of laughter as he bent down and kissed Bobby.

This time everything was softer and much more gentle. A gentle press of lips, a soft slide of skin against skin as Bobby guided Lewis down onto him, opening his legs so the fit was damned near perfect as anything could be. He caught a hand round the back of Lewis' neck, holding him in place as the kiss carried on and on and on.

Confirmation and reaffirmation.

Bobby hooked one ankle lightly over the back of Lewis' calf, not to hold in place, just to create more contact. More skin on skin. His hand found its way to

Lewis' and still the kiss went on until Bobby could feel his lips tingle. He tipped his head back, his knee pressing into Lewis' side, and looked at him through the awkward angle. "One day, after the war, you should grow your hair longer, below your collar."

"You think I'd look better that way?"

Bobby considered. "I think I'd like running my hands through it, holding onto it."

"Okay." Lewis smiled. "I'll grow it long. After the war. But I refuse to tie it back with a ribbon. I am not being a girl for you."

"Who wants a girl?" Bobby smoothed his hands appreciatively down Lewis' back, paying particular attention to each and every muscle. "I like your shoulders and arms and... Most of you, just as you are."

"Most of me?" Lewis licked up the column of Bobby's neck, pressing his nose into the flesh behind his ear. Bobby lay back and let him, hands flexing and sliding over Lewis' back.

"Apart from your legs."

"What's wrong with my legs?" Lewis didn't bother stopping as he ran his open mouth into the hollow at the base of Bobby's throat.

"They're too long," Bobby said with complete seriousness, as he pressed Lewis' head down and hooked his ankles higher up Lewis' legs. "They make you taller than me."

Lewis burst out laughing, the sound glorious and warm in the pale light from the small lamp. "God, I..." He lifted himself up on both hands, tipped his head to one side and smiled down. "I really do, Bobby."

"I do too," Bobby said, and he knew exactly what they both meant.

* * * *

Lewis walked into the mess with a face like thunder. Everyone watched as he got a cup of tea—his angry complaints about the lack of coffee ignored but noted, everyone thought he'd given up bothering long ago—and threw himself into a seat by an empty table at the far end of the large room.

Bobby raised an eyebrow but didn't say a word.

Lewis lifted the chair legs and let them repeatedly hit the ground, again and again, with a loud and annoying crack.

"For your sake I think it's just as well we're not flying this afternoon," Dennis said to Bobby. "It's better for the war effort if we keep you in one piece."

"You think I should go and talk to him?"

"I'd say emphatically no, not if you've any sense. But I don't think the linoleum is going to last long with treatment like that."

Lewis' chair slammed down again, even harder, and Bobby sighed as he got up.

"Good luck, old boy," Dennis called after him. "If you're not back in half an hour I'll send the medical chappies in after you."

Bobby detoured over to the serving station and managed to wangle a day-old piece of unidentifiable cake from the cook. He sat opposite Lewis and slid the plate over. "I brought you cake."

"Don't want it." Lewis folded his arms over his chest.

"Shut the fuck up. You always want cake." Bobby grinned as the plate bounced against Lewis' arm. Lewis glared at the plate for a moment then grabbed at it and took an enormous bite.

"It's stale." It didn't stop him eating the rest.

"Going to tell me what's the matter now?"

"Fucking nothing." He rubbed a hand over his face. "It's stupid."

"What is?"

Lewis sighed, long and dramatic. "The mail came in today and I got a pile of letters from my family. I swear to God, every damn one was moaning at me for staying here and not joining the US Army Air Force. My mom even said I was unpatriotic after 'all that our dear boys have suffered'."

"How about what everyone in England has suffered?"

"That's what I've been saying." Lewis leaned across the table, his hands spread wide in appeal for understanding. "But apparently that doesn't count as they're 'not one of us'." His mimicry of his mother's voice was vicious. "I thought we were all meant to be on the same side. Do you get this crap from your family?"

"Not really." Bobby shrugged. "I think they've given up on me. Remember I was fighting in Spain before this and they know how I feel." He suddenly gave an enormous grin. "They should, I told them enough times."

"Then you're lucky." Lewis huffed, but the anger had dissipated.

"So what are you going to do?" Bobby asked. "The USAAF would grab you any time, especially with the experience you have."

"And set me up with a bunch of airmen who are still wet behind the ears but think they're better than me just because they're older? No thanks." He pushed himself back until he was lying across his chair. "I'd know more than all of them but I bet they still wouldn't listen to me."

"And your family?"

"Fuck them," he said, huffing. "No, I don't mean that. They don't understand but I'm not going to bother explaining anymore. No one is going to tell me what to do."

"Except Roger." Bobby smiled over at him, small and mischievous. "And the Wing Commander. And Bomber Command and the bosses in London and Winston Churchill and—"

"Shut up." Lewis leaned over and swiped him around the head, but he was grinning as well now.

"So you'll listen to them?"

"Yeah, I guess so," Lewis admitted.

"Just not your family?"

"No."

"And me? Which side do I fall on?"

Again Lewis folded his arms across his chest, staring at Bobby as though he were a very, very stupid child. "You, I always listen to, even over the bosses."

Bobby smiled warmly. "But not over Roger?"

"Hell, no." Lewis grinned back. "Have you seen Roger fly? You're a good navigator but that man is a master in the cockpit. Only yesterday he had his Mosquito..."

Bobby stopped listening and simply watched the excitement on Lewis' face.

* * * *

March 1942

Another early morning briefing for another operation. Bobby looked around the room and realized that everyone was as scared as he was. It was only sensible to be scared when the mission had been arranged in a hurry and was voluntary. Voluntary? Bobby couldn't remember many of those.

The operation was to hit the Gestapo headquarters in Reims, France. Both of those things had everyone worried, even before they heard the details. The details didn't reassure. Wing Commander Stockton told them how local resistance fighters had been captured and they were currently being held at the headquarters where, no doubt, they would be forced to tell everything they knew.

He explained — his face a nasty shade of gray — that they knew a lot — too much. Details of local operations, the identities of those further along the resistance chain, even planned Allied operations. They couldn't be allowed to jeopardize all the work they'd already done. The headquarters would be bombed and the men silenced, as they would want.

Stockton went on, making sure they understood the danger. "This mission is going to need supreme precision bombing. But before that can happen you have to get there. That means halfway across occupied France."

This wasn't an operation anyone wanted to undertake but its importance was obvious.

"What do you think?" Lewis asked Bobby quietly. "Should we do it?"

"They're going to die anyway," Bobby said, his face taut and pale. "At least let's give them the honor of going with their secrets. Let it mean something."

Lewis paused for a moment then nodded, before starting to take notes on the details.

Roger would be in command with his new navigator — although Bobby would act as lead navigator—along with three new crews. When he heard that, Bobby protested that they weren't ready for something so dangerous and complex but Wing Commander Stockton became tight-lipped and indignant. "They have to learn that no one is indispensable. Or are you questioning my orders?"

Bobby shook his head, put on his cap and walked from the room, his back ramrod straight. He could feel it—this wasn't going to go right or easy. But it still had to be done.

* * * *

"God damn it," Lewis growled when enemy aircraft intercepted them as soon as they crossed the shoreline of France. "You were so damned careful to keep as far away from the towns as possible but they've still found us."

"We can outrun them," Bobby said, but it wasn't to be that easy. There was heavy fire both at the coast and what felt like every step inland. As they got closer to the target the flak got worse with bigger guns with more accurate operators. There were also increasing numbers of enemy planes that, at one point, seemed to come at them from every direction.

"Steady, skip," Bobby said to Lewis, when he started getting flustered, although the adrenaline was beginning to bite at Bobby's belly as well. This was as bad as anything they'd encountered before.

Lewis exhaled noisily through his nose and, concentrating hard, kept them securely on course.

But the enemy action didn't stop. They lost two of the new crews before they even caught sight of Reims. Bobby watched them go down but didn't say a word.

There was a job to be done and now they owed it to the lost crews to do it right.

Eventually they got there but coming in over the target meant passing gun emplacements. Roger went first and it was a close call. He pulled up hard and Bobby could see machine-gun holes along the back of his fuselage. But Roger, being the leader they all admired, had still managed to drop his bombs. It appeared to be an accurate hit but they couldn't tell and they had to be sure, very sure.

"I'm going to go in low and make sure we can see exactly what we need to hit," Lewis said, already making the maneuver. He kept the airplane low and careful and… They dropped their bombs at the right moment and got out of the way as quickly as possible. But they were caught, a fireball running over the top of the plane, leaving a hole the size of a hand span, blackening the body and fusing the glass of the cockpit.

Bobby felt like his heart was in his mouth for a moment but then his training kicked in. "We're okay, skip. We're lucky the flames didn't catch hold." He looked over his shoulder, trying to make out the scene. "Let's hope that did the job."

The last remaining new aircrew went in next and their timing wasn't quite right. Their plane disappeared in the plume of smoke and fire and they were lost from view for a moment.

"Fuck," Bobby spat the word out, as he stretched round again to see for as long as he could. Just as Lewis was about to accelerate hard the others came out of the smoke. "They're with us," he called over the radio to no one in particular, his relief palpable.

Then the whole group of planes got out of there as fast as the Mosquitoes' engines would take them, heading for England.

But still their luck didn't turn and the trip back was a bumpy ride, worse than the outward journey had been. "Word must have spread all along the German lines," Lewis said. "They seem to be expecting us whichever route you take."

"I know." Bobby studied the map again, every muscle in his body held tight. "We can outrun the fighter planes but we're being pushed toward guns on the ground."

"You tell me where you want me to go and I'll get us there," Lewis said. "You, me and Betty – best team in the squadron."

Bobby loved his optimism and did his damnedest to live up to it. They swerved, twisted and maneuvered every way they knew, rising to maximum altitude where they could, ducking low when necessary. Even so the new pilot, Billy, got hit under the back wing, which affected his control. The flak had also damaged his rear landing gear but that was one thing Bobby insisted they could put off worrying about that until they were the right side of the Channel.

All three aircraft were now limping along. The wind kept catching the hole on the top of Betty and Bobby was pretty sure it got a little bigger each time he looked. The opening was starting to affect stability and the plane shook and rolled in the air. Lewis had to fight for control.

Billy's voice came nervously over the radio every few minutes – the kid was twenty and terrified. Both Roger and Bobby reassured him as Lewis kept his death grip on the controls. They had enough fuel to get back to base, and there'd be people there to make sure he landed safely without the back wheel. Billy was scared and he had the right to be, but Bobby was sure that things would be okay. They were nearly home now.

Bobby was astonished that it was Roger who didn't make it home. He was caught not concentrating as they neared the outskirts of a small town. The anti-aircraft guns ripped through his starboard wing making it impossible for him to fly. He rose as high as he could before gliding down, trying to find a field to land safely in.

He even had time to say goodbye and wish them well before he landed. Lewis slowed but there was nothing anyone could do, they needed to get out of there as quickly as they could. Bobby saw two figures climb out of the plane but he couldn't tell who got to them first, whether it was the lorry loads of Germans driving frantically along the narrow country lane or the local farmers running across country.

At least Roger and his navigator were alive.

They were silent as they crossed the Channel, the water only feet below them. They stayed that way until they got near the base, then Lewis talked Billy through the emergency landing procedures. Billy had known them—they'd been drummed into him. But fear had a way of making a man forget if he wasn't used to the feeling.

Both planes landed as well as could be expected and all four crew walked away. Bobby patted everyone's back as they headed for debriefing. He couldn't think of the right thing to say but hoped they'd know what he meant.

Even Leading Aircraftman Tilly admitted it was a better result than might have been expected. He glanced at Lewis then up at Betty and added, "Repairs will take a long, long time."

* * * *

"So?" Lewis asked as Bobby came out of the Wing Commander's office. "Who's the new Squadron Leader?"

Bobby patted his pockets, looking for a cigarette. He didn't actually want one but he'd been in debriefing and meetings for hours and he was tired. Everyone was dog-tired. Even Lewis, who always stayed more cheerful and positive than anyone else, looked ready to drop. "I am."

"You are?" Lewis fell into step beside him down the corridor. "That would be great except you've turned it down a dozen times already."

"This time it was made clear it wasn't voluntary. I was ordered to take the promotion."

"Can they do that?"

"They can do anything they like." He stopped suddenly and held his hand out. "Give me a goddamn cigarette." Lewis lit two and passed one over before sucking deeply on his own. Bobby did the same. "I think the whole thing is punishment for arguing with him before the operation—I shouldn't have done that in front of other people."

Lewis leaned back against the wall, cigarette at his lips. "I know you don't like the situation but it's a good thing and the Commander knows that."

"A good thing?"

"Come on, admit it, you'll make a great Squadron Leader. Everyone respects you, from the cook and the ground crews to the pilots. You have great tactical knowledge, you're good under pressure and you don't take crap from anyone."

"I don't want to be a Squadron Leader, I want to fight."

"And you know that argument doesn't work here. You'll be flying just as much as you ever did, doing everything you ever have. Only now you'll be able to correct mistakes and give orders. Tact never was your strongest point." Lewis pushed away and started walking again.

"I don't want to be responsible for anyone else," Bobby persisted.

"Tough shit, you'll be good at this."

"But I don't want to give orders."

"Well, you have to take them so, like I said, tough shit. This will be good for the rest of us and the war. The Commander's no fool. Only downside I can see is now you're, what? Three ranks higher than me?" He leaned closer, voice dropping. "We can play that game in bed, but I'll still outrank you in the air."

"Not three." Bobby fought against the heating of his cheeks. "You're getting promoted as well. You're going up two ranks, you're now a Flight Lieutenant."

"I…" Lewis slowed. "Oh wow, even my mom will be impressed."

"It's about time. You should have got a promotion ages ago. Roger held back because he didn't want anyone to notice you and move you on somewhere else. Now he's sitting the rest of the war out in a POW camp he hasn't got a say anymore."

"You're still one rank higher than me, and you'll actually be my direct Commanding Officer. That's new. I'm kind of glad that wasn't the case when we first started." Lewis slung an arm casually round

Bobby's neck, bending so he was close to Bobby's ear. "But it means you can give orders in bed."

"I don't…"

"But you'd like to." Lewis grinned. "Squadron Leader Davenport."

* * * *

Operations had to be canceled while the aircraft were fixed. It was a lot of work but that meant there was time to train the new crews. They'd had all the instruction the RAF thought necessary but Bobby wanted them to have more real-time experience in the air.

"Really?" Lewis had queried on behalf of the new men.

"Yes," Bobby insisted. "They need to fly complicated maneuvers over as difficult terrain as I can find. I want them at the stage where actions and reactions became automatic, so let's get them chasing each other as though in combat. I want them coming out of the sun, from behind clouds, flying extremely low and pulling up hard when we call 'flak ahead'." He paused for a moment, looking at the new guys sitting outside the briefing room in their pristine flying gear. "I want them as ready as they can be."

"Okay." Lewis nodded.

Everyone understood the reasoning behind being as ready as you could be.

Bobby thought they had about a week before the squadron would be given the green light as operational again. Which meant, with several aircraft out of service, they had to fly at all hours. But he knew that was a good thing as well, since night flying was a very different skill.

Once Bobby had persuaded him of the need for it, Lewis had a great time. He tried out all the new planes, showing off as he chased the less experienced pilots across the sky and attempted to disorient the navigators. It wasn't, he explained, that he wanted to give Betty up, more that he wanted all the Mosquitoes for himself, just like he had since he'd first seen them.

Bobby shook his head, watching as Lewis raced an older pilot to the planes arranged on the grass, before getting in and taking off.

"Good to see someone is having fun," Dennis said. "I'm getting a new navigator because the old one has pissed off to fly heavy bombers. The whole thing smacks of treachery to me."

"Don't tell Lewis," Bobby urged. "He'd see anyone leaving the Mosquitoes as more than a traitor."

"He's awfully keen, isn't he?" Dennis smiled indulgently. "Good job he's a damn good pilot as well—it would become more than a little trying otherwise."

"He's all right." Bobby shrugged. "He puts up with a lot."

"Like his superior being his navigator? It's a funny old world in the RAF. I say…" Dennis stepped out farther onto the airfield. "That's an awfully strange noise to be coming from a Mossie."

Bobby heard it too, the sound of an engine… He wasn't sure but it didn't seem right. No, he did know—that was the noise of an engine failing. Just then the noise stopped and the engine with it. The plane seemed to hover for a moment but then Lewis must have managed to catch an air current and he started to glide in toward the landing strip.

His attempt was good, masterful even, but the plane landed heavily, almost immediately tipping to one side as it slid across the grass. Time seemed to go in slow motion as the inevitable momentum took the machine farther off course.

Bobby could visualize the plane hitting the side of a storage building before it happened. Could see it catch alight before the acrid smell of burning fuel reached his nose. For that brief moment it was as if life had stopped and he could see the future before events took place. Could see them, but do nothing to stop them.

Once, when he was small, there'd been an accident while he was playing with his brother. They'd been on their bikes and his brother had hit a big stone sticking out of the ground. Bobby had known what would happen next, could see it in his mind. His brother would go over the handlebars and land hard on his head. He'd be cut and broken, would need to be stitched at the hospital. Events had happened in his mind before they'd taken place but he'd been unable to move from the spot. Frozen and ineffective as a spectator to a film.

This time he was running long before the crash actually occurred and the fire started.

The heat was fierce but the plane wasn't engulfed, not yet. One wing was crumpled into a heap of torn and twisted wood, the round circles of the RAF symbol still showing clearly on a splintered piece. Even now it seemed iconic, something that stood for so much. Iconic and incongruous as it lay detached from the rest of the aircraft.

They had time—not much, but enough. Bobby wasn't sure he believed in God anymore but he started praying.

Lewis loved the Mosquito—the plane was his passion, his life. It couldn't become his coffin.

People were speeding toward the plane from all directions but Bobby was one of the earliest to arrive. Even so, Tilly was first up onto the remaining wing, smashing the glass at the top of the cockpit to pull out the crew as the flames licked in from the other side. The new navigator was first and that was... That was... Bobby just wanted him out of the way. Then they could get to Lewis.

Between them, he and Tilly unfastened Lewis' restraining straps, fighting against the fire inside the cockpit, and pulled him up and out. It wasn't easy. Lewis was semi-conscious, his size difficult to manage in the tight confines. His hands flailed in the air and Bobby noticed that he'd lost a glove somewhere along the line. The backs of his fingers were black with soot and sweat, the skin torn as though he'd been desperately scratching to break his way out.

Lewis caught hold of Bobby's sleeve. "Bobby?"

"It's okay, I've got you. We're going to get you out of here and somewhere safe."

Lewis didn't say anymore but he didn't let go.

Quickly they dragged him across the wing, down onto the ground and away from the burning aircraft. They rolled him onto his belly as the ambulance pulled up alongside. It was only then that Bobby saw the damage to the back of Lewis' jacket. The thick leather was still smoldering with fragments of material breaking off and falling away, and the smell was awful.

Bobby knew what that meant. If a flying jacket was that burned so was the man underneath.

He pushed the panic, and his breakfast, back down and helped lift Lewis onto a stretcher.

Not dead.

He kept repeating the words over and over in his head. Not dead and not as burned as some. He'd seen the Battle of Britain pilots, proud in their smart uniforms, their faces melted and unrecognizable. Ears and noses missing, mouths a scar along with the rest of their flesh.

Not dead. Dear God, not dying. Please God, not dying or... Not burned so that even his own mother wouldn't know him.

Things could have been so much worse. Things could have been...

But it was Lewis. Bobby's fingers curled into Lewis' collar, the knuckles and tendons so tight he knew they were hurting even though he couldn't feel the pain.

All Bobby wanted to do was hold onto him until the doctors pronounced him fit and Bobby could have him back. But that wasn't allowed. The ambulance was standing ready, its doors wide open, engine running, driver shouting things Bobby couldn't hear. He wasn't sure if he was helping or getting in the way as the stretcher was lifted into the back. All he knew was that he'd have to let go in a moment. He'd have to let go of Lewis' collar, let go of Lewis.

He wasn't sure he could move, wasn't sure he was physically capable of straightening his fingers, of pulling his hands away.

Lewis was face down, his body a long line of RAF blue, of leather jacket, of messy hair. The smell of burning was thick in the air, clouds of dirty, black smoke that sat on Bobby's skin, coated his throat, got into his eyes. Shouting and noise, frantic activity all around him, heat from the fire—but he couldn't register any of it.

The whole world had contracted to a silent bubble containing only Lewis and himself.

Now all he had to do was open his fingers. Open his fingers and take control back again. Open his fingers and remember who and what he was.

He couldn't do it. Not even as voices shouted at him, angry and frustrated. Not until Dennis' hand came down on his shoulder, squeezing much too hard. Then he let go.

There was a war on after all.

Chapter Five

1st April 1942

Bobby sat on the hard chair in the corridor, tap, tap, tapping out a rhythmless noise on the wooden floor with his foot. He'd been waiting over half an hour and the pressure was becoming unbearable. Lewis was behind that door. Lewis, whom he'd heard reports about but hadn't seen.

Lewis, who'd been in surgery, kept sedated and was now awake. Awake and Bobby wasn't there to see him, to reassure him.

Wasn't there to reassure himself that Lewis really was alive.

Lewis, who he hadn't seen for three days. Not since he'd been stopped from climbing into the back of the ambulance. The last glimpse he'd had of Lewis had been of a blackened, smoldering flying jacket as the door was closed on him.

Unconsciously his hands balled into fists and he thought about hitting someone, something.

A nurse passed by him. "I'm sure it won't be long now," she said briskly. "Doctor's nearly done. Would you like more tea?"

More fucking tea. Just about the last thing he needed. He could add the drink to the collection of cold cups already on the window sill. He scowled, not bothering to answer, and went back to his tapping.

He waited another ten minutes before the white-coated doctor finally came out, surrounded by a flurry of nurses. "Ah, you must be Winters' Commanding Officer," the doctor said, holding out his hand.

"That's right." Bobby shook hands. "His CO and navigator. How is he? Can I go in and see him now?"

"Sorry about the wait, old chap, we were making an assessment of his wounds, seeing what we can do for him."

"And?" Bobby felt breathless, fear suddenly clutching at his belly.

"A bit bumpy at first but things aren't as bad as we first thought. He's going to need skin grafts across his left shoulder, down along the blade, but I'm sure he'll get back full use. Nasty scarring, mind you, and it'll take a few operations, which will inevitably be painful, but he's very lucky."

"Lucky? Not so lucky for him or me," Bobby said, looking away.

"For you?" The doctor stared at him quizzically.

Bobby shook himself. He couldn't make a mistake like that, not now. "He's a damn good pilot, my pilot. The squadron needs him."

"You'll get him back." The doctor was already turning to leave. "Might take a while but he'll fly again and he is lucky, extraordinarily so. He took his glove off — a mistake like that could have cost him the use of his hand, has for other poor souls I've seen. He's lucky the flames didn't reach that far."

Bobby closed his eyes for a brief moment, exhaling softly, then watched the doctor's back as he walked away. Lucky. They were lucky. He'd have to remember that.

He gathered up his cap and coat and pushed open the door to the ward. A nurse immediately directed him to a bed at the far end. Men were lying in, or sitting next to, the other beds he passed. Some had limbs missing—a leg here, an arm there. The really unlucky ones had smooth flat sheets where their legs should have been. Many were burned, a few horrifically so. Others had new grafts, the skin looking alien, unnatural. But ears and noses could be rebuilt, even faces. Eyes not.

Yes, they were lucky.

Then he was at Lewis' bed. He stopped at the end, looking down. Lewis lay on his belly, white sheet pulled up just above his waist, a thick dressing covering him from under his hairline, down his neck, flooding out over his left shoulder, the top of his arm, to disappear under the covers. His hair was singed, the frazzled ends still curling blackly, his skin dark underneath. But most was still intact and the skin he could see was still smooth and perfect, except for the odd cuts and bruises.

Lucky.

He felt a rush of emotion sweep over him, relief nowhere near as strong as the love.

"Is someone there?" Lewis tried to crane his neck round to see, crying out as the pain in his shoulder hit. "Fucking hell," he said, gasping through the hurt. "Don't just stand there—move so I can see you."

Bobby pushed along beside the window to get to the head of the bed, hanging his coat on the back of the chair as he pulled it up close and perched on the edge. "Is that any way to talk to your Squadron Leader?" He smiled down at Lewis, hand reaching out without thinking. "Lucky I make exceptions for the wounded."

"Bobby." Lewis' eyes went round, his voice softening. "I thought you were never coming."

"I tried, tried real hard, but they wouldn't let me. The doctors didn't want anyone contaminating your wounds."

"You should have told them you've already infected me." Lewis gave a poor attempt at a smile, the corners of his lips curling over the pain. He had a bruise over his left eye, there were numerous small cuts and bruises down the side of his face and his top lip was swollen. But all Bobby could see was that he was alive.

Alive and talking and… He gave a small sigh of relief before looking up to scan the ward quickly. There was no one watching, not for a moment. He reached out, brushing the hair off Lewis' forehead, hand cupping his cheek, his fingers smoothing over skin. "God, I…" He tried, but the words faltered, caught in his throat. "They wouldn't tell me anything at first and I didn't know how you were. They wouldn't even tell me where you were and…" His voice cracked as he tied down his emotions as tight as he could manage.

"Don't worry." Lewis caught his wrist, holding on tight. "I'm okay. Or at least I will be."

There was a sudden noise from the other end of the ward, voices raised in argument, and Bobby had no choice but to pull his hand away. He sat up straighter, trying to appear like a senior officer, but he couldn't help pulling his chair closer until his knees brushed against the bed frame. He inhaled sharply, holding the breath before letting it go slowly, his gaze never leaving Lewis'. "How are you feeling?"

"Honestly?" Lewis sank back into the pillow, angling his head and his fingertips a fraction of an inch from Bobby's thigh. "Everything fucking hurts. So bad at times I could scream, that I do scream. But I can't complain, there are so many in here worse off than me."

"Ask for some morphine. That's not complaining, that's just being sensible."

"They try to give me some but I won't take too much."

"For God's sake, why not?" Bobby asked, concerned.

"Because I can't think straight if I do. Can't think, don't know what's real. I get hallucinations, I..." He twisted against the sheets, lips thinning to a gray line. "I thought I saw you in the plane, thought you were dying, and all I could smell was burning flesh."

"Lewis," Bobby said, everything he felt rolled into the one word as he pushed forward, desperate to hold, to help, to reassure. "Hell, I wish there was something I could say, something I could do. I can't even fucking touch you."

"Touching would be nice." Lewis ran a finger along the seam of Bobby's uniform, quick but not furtive, not this time. "But I'm better now I've seen you, even if I'd prefer it if you could get in with me."

"I can't see them letting us get away with that. Maybe I should retrain as a nurse, then I could give you a bed bath." Bobby tried to smile.

"I'm going to hold you to that. You just wait and see—when I'm out of here I'm going to demand one." Lewis looked up, one hand resting, out of sight, against the side of Bobby's knee.

"So what have they done up to now?" Bobby asked.

"I've had one op," Lewis said, pressing his tongue against the front of his teeth and frowning. "I think that was mostly to clear everything out, cut away the burnt, dead skin and see what they could save. The actual operation wasn't bad, neither was waking up. I was on so many meds I couldn't remember much. Then they wore off and…" He reached up, rubbing at his face. "I don't like it much when they take the bandages off to check things. That isn't fun."

"Get them to give you something, there must be a different kind of pain relief you can take."

"Nothing works quite like morphine," Lewis said, ruefully. "But at least my hand seems okay." He lifted the hand that had lost its glove. The skin was blackened in places, burnt in others with nasty-looking scabs forming, but Lewis flexed his fingers, balling and opening his fist. It worked just fine.

"You really are damn lucky."

"Yeah, I know. I've seen guys with their fingers fused together. I can't quite feel properly but the doctor said, when it heals completely, the hand should be back to normal." He stared up at Bobby, his eyes dark. "There are things I want to feel."

"Then I'm damn lucky as well."

"Do me a favor?" Lewis asked, the expression on his face changing.

"Of course, anything."

"Write to my parents, tell them what's happened. The doctor here was going to send them a report but I asked him to wait. I want them to hear the news from you."

"You know I will. After all, I'm supposed to, as your Squadron Leader."

"Yeah but..." Lewis eased himself in the bed, his face flashing with pain and concentration for a moment. "Don't tell them as my CO, tell them as my friend, now you've seen me, spoken to me. You know I'm going to be all right, that I'm still me. Tell them that."

"I will, I'll write tonight. Do they know anything about me?"

"I've written, told them that you're my navigator, my friend. I..." Lewis smiled, soft and small. "I'm pretty sure my momma has the idea that you're important to me."

"She knows? About what you are?"

"No, not officially," Lewis said with feeling. "But it's like you told me once before—don't force them to know, to acknowledge anything. It's easier that way. But... Yeah, I think she knows, and from what she's said in her letters, she's read between the lines of mine. She knows." He laughed, short but bright. "She must, I write about you a lot... A hell of a lot."

"It's nice you can do that, I think." Bobby tried to laugh with him.

"You can't?"

Bobby grimaced, more in that one expression than he normally gave away. "My mom sat me down when I was about eighteen, and told me not to get too close to other boys. She said it wasn't natural." He shrugged, trying to dismiss the events of years before. "I was careful not to mention anyone too much after that. She made sure I knew where we both stood."

"My daddy's like that." Lewis' voice turned somber. "Wanted me to be a 'real man'. When I was younger I even used to make up girls to tell him about. That's pretty lame of me, don't you think?"

"We all do what we have to do to get by. There's nothing wrong in that. Anyway, we're lucky," Bobby said quietly. "We managed to find each other."

"And we're a lucky pairing." Lewis carried on after Bobby frowned. "Just like you said, we're a lucky pairing. We'll be okay as long as we're together. That's why I got hurt, because we weren't together."

"That's not right," Bobby said. "We thought at first you crashed because there was a problem with the engine, but that wasn't the fault. It turned out that the new kid working as a mechanic had made basic mistakes and you were running on the dirty fuel at the bottom of the tank. It was a stupid error and the CO disciplined him."

"No, no." Lewis shook his head. "That may have been the cause but it wasn't the reason."

"That doesn't make sense."

"We're a lucky pairing. I crashed because I was flying with a different navigator, not you." Lewis spoke with such complete certainty that he made the words sound like a proven fact, one that couldn't be disputed.

But the idea still took Bobby's breath away. "That's… You can't think like that."

"Of course I can. I have to because it's the truth."

"No, there was dirt in the fuel and—"

"Doesn't matter what you say, I'm right and you know it," Lewis cut him short.

"But—"

"Think about it, how many tight scrapes have we been in? How many times have we been hit but not shot down? Hell, how many times have we crawled back to base on the last drip of fuel, when the display panel had been registering empty since the coast?

We've been in much worse circumstances than what happened, but we've always pulled through."

"We've been lu —" This time Bobby stopped himself.

"Go on, say it, we've been lucky. That's because we are lucky. It has to be true because you told me."

Bobby thought back — he had said something like that. But he sure hadn't meant the words the way Lewis was taking them. "I said it to make you feel safer, because you were scared."

"I know that. Doesn't stop it from being true, though," Lewis said with finality.

"I..." Bobby caught his bottom lip between his teeth for a moment, niggling at the flesh. "I don't know what to say to that."

"Don't say anything, just know I'm right."

"If it helps, if you want to think... Hell, sure, why not? Yeah, we're lucky."

"Doesn't matter if you can't admit it out loud." Lewis gave a small, tight smile. "It's true, which means we're going to make it through this war because I'm not flying with anyone other than you."

"You can't say things like that. You don't have any control over... Oh fuck it." Bobby gave up and attempted to smile along with him. "We're lucky, you remember that while you're lying in bed and we'll talk about it again when you're better."

"Talk all you like but I'm not flying with anyone else." Lewis' grin was wide, but there was steel behind his words, in his eyes. "And neither are you."

Bobby knew the smile slipped from his face, replaced by a serious, dark look. "You're going to be out of action for at least a few months, I can't just sit on my butt and wait for you."

"Yes, you can." Lewis' face was set just as firm, the smile long gone. "Ask for a leave of absence."

"Don't be stupid, no one just gets time off."

"Ask for compassionate leave."

"For what?" Bobby shook his head, bending over so that their faces were close. "Because my homosexual lover is in the hospital? That's ridiculous."

"Then tell them your mom is seriously ill, something, anything." Lewis tried to push himself up, ignoring the pain. "Just don't fucking fly."

"They aren't giving anyone time off, you know that. I couldn't get back to the States even if I wanted to and…" Bobby stopped, appalled at the gray, sweat-dampened look on Lewis' face. Only half an hour ago he'd just been so glad that Lewis was alive. He knew Lewis wasn't well enough for a row like this. He deliberately calmed himself before reaching over to ease Lewis back onto the pillow. "We'll talk about this later, when you're feeling better. Next time I come and see you."

"Okay." Again Lewis relaxed back onto the bed. "Just as long as you don't fly between now and then."

Bobby pressed his lips tightly together and didn't say a word.

"Bobby?" Lewis looked at him, eyes a little less sure, a little more concerned. "Promise me." The words weren't a request. He caught Bobby's wrist. "Promise me."

"I can't," Bobby said softly.

"You can and you will because you have to." Lewis' fingers tightened painfully, his voice constricting along with them.

"I can't, you know that." Bobby leaned closer still, aiming his words just for Lewis but conscious of the rest of the ward. "There are raids planned, our best pilot is out injured and —"

"Bobby," Lewis said desperately, pulling Bobby in even closer. "You can't fly."

"I have to. I'm the fucking Squadron Leader. I can't bail on the men and I don't want to."

"No, no." There was an edge of hysteria in Lewis' voice. One that was growing along with the volume. "You can't. You'll die and I couldn't stand that, not when I've just found you. I need you."

"Shhh," Bobby tried to pry his hand away from Lewis' grip to pat at his arm. "I'm not going to die." He deliberately lowered his voice, hoping that Lewis would follow. "Everything's going to be fine but I have to fly."

"No..."

"Shhh," Bobby tried again, as though soothing a frightened animal. "You're on a lot of medication, you've got things muddled. You're taking the whole lucky pairing thing too literally. But I have to fight, I want to."

"Take a desk job if you have to, you just can't—"

"I can," Bobby said, sounding more like the authoritative Commanding Officer he was. "There's a war on, remember. It's too important to ignore. I'm going to do my part, not just sit at a desk ordering other poor suckers to do things I won't."

"What about us?"

Bobby sat back, watching Lewis closely. "I don't suppose Hitler cares about us, or the thousands of other couples torn apart by the war. We're not important, not compared to what we're fighting against."

"Yes, we are. We are." Lewis' voice rose to a yell as he pushed himself up, trying to get off the bed.

At that point the nurses and doctors came running with their restraining hands and sedatives. Bobby stood back against the wall, face ashen, scared beyond belief at what he'd done, and watched as Lewis was forced back down. Watched as he was injected, fighting every step of the way. Watched blood seep from under the white bandages, as pain spread across his face.

Watched until Lewis slumped into unconsciousness and was manhandled like a slab of meat on the bed as an edge of the dressing was lifted.

Then he saw the damage underneath. Red, raw flesh, looking more like something found on a butcher's counter than a man, crusted in places, black and charred. Meat cooked too quickly over an open flame. He'd seen that, back in Texas. He hadn't thought he'd ever see the like on a man, a friend. On the man he loved.

He stood there while the doctor talked to him, explaining how the drugs Lewis had been given made him act irrationally, out of character. That he'd be fine, how everything was perfectly normal, in the circumstances.

In the circumstances. Bobby didn't think the doctor understood the circumstances, not at all.

He nodded when he was advised to come back again, assured that Lewis would be more rational then. Told he would be allowed in whenever he could manage the time, seeing as he was on active service. He nodded again, collecting his things before he left.

He took one last look back. Lewis was face down in the bed, his mouth scarcely clear of the sheets, his back uncovered except for the dressing, one arm hanging down off the bed. Bobby had a sudden image, clear in his mind, of Lewis laid out in exactly the same position in a small attic boarding house room, all loose-limbed and easy after hours spent fucking. Of himself licking along Lewis' spine, exploring all that skin with mouth and hands. Of Lewis' soft, happy sounds of laughter.

For a moment the breath caught in his throat and he thought he just might scream. He closed his eyes and made a silent promise to Lewis that he'd be back as soon as he could manage it. Then he shut the door quietly behind him as he left.

* * * *

It was nearly a week before Bobby could get back to the hospital—a frantic, bloody week. One that had contained operations, bombs and destruction, but also something else. Again he waited outside the ward, this time only for a few minutes, before he was allowed in, clutching his brown paper bag of apples. Nancy, in the mess, had told him they were the type of thing you took to someone in hospital. She'd also been the one to find them on the black market.

Lewis was once more lying on his belly, but now he had a folded page from a newspaper held in his good hand and a thin white shirt covering his back. Bobby knew what lay underneath. Right now he didn't want to be reminded.

"Hello," he said, finding the seat next to the bed. "You look better than when I last saw you."

Lewis stopped, dropped the paper, and simply stared at Bobby for a moment. "Hello to you too, it's good to see you. I…" His mouth stayed open, almost working as though there was more to come.

"Are you feeling better?" Bobby held out the bag, showing Lewis the contents before putting the apples on the side table.

"Yeah, I guess. They have me on different pain medication, one that doesn't make my head feel like it's full of cotton wool, even if it doesn't work as well." He shifted in the bed, angling himself toward Bobby. "You picked the right day to come because I have my next skin graft operation tomorrow. I won't be so good then, and they have a whole series planned."

"But that's good, isn't it? About the ops, it means you're getting better?"

Still Lewis was staring. His face full of concentration and Bobby wasn't sure what the expression meant.

"Yeah, I guess." Then, suddenly, Lewis smiled, soft and small. "You don't look so good, though, you're gray round the edges."

"Been a tough few days." Bobby admitted. "I... I missed you." He ducked his head, hardly looking at Lewis. "It's not the same without you there."

"Told you," Lewis said confidently. "Doesn't matter, though, as long as you don't fly."

Bobby stayed silent, his head still lowered.

"You haven't been, have you?" Lewis pushed himself up, swinging his legs round to sit on the edge of the bed, his face contorting with pain for a flash. "Have you?" he demanded.

"Please." Bobby could hear the begging tone himself. "Don't start again, not now when I've only just got here."

"You have, haven't you?" There was defeat in his voice, mixed with the anger Bobby had half expected. "Couldn't you have stopped? Just for a while."

"No, I really couldn't, I..." Bobby twisted his fingers together for a moment before inhaling sharply, steeling himself. "I need to fight. I want to. I can't stop now because things are too important. Before you say it, we're important as well, more important than I ever thought possible but this... This is about nation fighting nation, the whole world. The war is about good versus evil and I have to fight."

"What's happened?" Lewis said, tone much softer than anything Bobby had hoped for.

"Nothing. At least nothing important, I..." Again Bobby ran out of words.

"Don't lie to me." Lewis leaned in closer. "I can see it's a lie. I know you too well. Please, don't treat me like a fool or, worse, an invalid. You're too important to me. I need to know what's happened to you."

"It... I..." Bobby licked at suddenly dry lips, pushing the air in and out of his lungs as he ran a hand through his slicked hair. "Things went wrong. I couldn't concentrate with a different pilot. I was watching him rather than leading the squadron and..."

"Tell me." Lewis laid an encouraging hand on his knee, just for a moment.

"I made a mistake, no, a few of them, a whole catalog. Not enough to get anyone killed but it was a close call. Much too close. You know what it's like up there, you have to be totally focused." He glanced up, eyes sharp on Lewis. "I was thinking about you, here," he said, honestly, appalled at himself. "I messed up and I can't do that."

"But you said no one's dead? The planes? Betty?"

"They're all okay. The CO doesn't know what went wrong that time but..." He clutched Lewis' wrist, for once not caring who could see. "I do. It was too close. Much, much too close."

"Hold on, hold on," Lewis reassured, his fingers gripping tight as Bobby fought for control. "It's all going to be okay." He twisted so their knees were touching and pressed into the contact as he brushed his fingertips over the back of Bobby's hand, softly. "Come on," he encouraged. "Don't break down now."

Bobby sucked in one ragged breath after another, concentrating on Lewis' face until he was under a semblance of control. But the knowledge was still there, the horror of what he'd done. Of what might have happened.

Lewis patted his hand again, glancing back at the ward. "Pull the curtain around the bed, let's give ourselves a modicum of privacy. Go on." He pushed at Bobby. "We can always say we were discussing something secret, if anyone asks. They won't, though, they're all RAF and they know about keeping things hush-hush."

Bobby did as he was told, glad to be moving and not having to think what to do for once. He went back to his chair, looking at Lewis for a moment before giving in and hugging him. He hesitated for a second, unsure where to put his hands, what he could touch, before resting one on Lewis' thigh. The other went up into his hair, holding on tight as he inhaled Lewis' smell, pressed his mouth close to get a hint of his taste.

He held on too long, too tight and he knew it. But there was nothing he could do, not right then.

Lewis was the one who eased him away, guiding him back in his chair with a gentle hand, which he left on Bobby's knee. "Now tell me how bad it was."

"We were on an operation, nine Mosquitoes and... I wasn't concentrating. I didn't pick up on things I should have. I wasn't giving orders quickly enough. It could have been a disaster."

"But it wasn't." Lewis stroked over the rough uniform covering Bobby's leg.

"No, Dennis covered for me, he's had to a couple of times and that's never happened before. He's never needed to."

"How did the other men take it?"

"I don't think any of the new guys noticed, but a couple of the old ones did. Afterward, they looked at me strangely and asked after you." Bobby shook his head. "I'm not sure what they thought."

"I'm pretty sure some know about us. The rest will put it down to the navigator–pilot bond, with the added effect of us being the only Americans around. But either way that isn't good." Lewis tipped his head, studying Bobby. "You said the old man doesn't know what happened. Did he say anything?"

"Not about that incident specifically, but Wing Commander Stockton's no fool. He told me after that flight that I was off. He's putting that down to the shock of you getting hurt. He's still not impressed, though. He…" Once more Bobby ground to a halt, his gaze pleading with Lewis. But even he didn't know if he was asking for understanding or something else. "He called me into his office, gave me the biggest tongue-lashing of my life."

"Bobby?" Lewis' voice was tight.

"I can't argue with him because he's right. I needed a good kick up the ass before I got someone killed."

"You won't do that."

"I came a damn sight too close and half the men know it."

"They trust you."

"No, even Dennis just nodded when I got back from the boss's office. But…" He inhaled slowly, feeling the skin on his face pull tight. "Deserved doesn't stop it being humiliating. The Commander told me I was bringing discredit on myself. That if I didn't 'buck my ideas up, laddie', I'd bring disgrace on the squadron and all Americans, for Christ's sake. He threatened me with all sorts of things."

"Like what?"

"Like he'd talk to Bomber Command, get me transferred."

"Where?" Lewis said, low, questioning. "A desk job? Maybe that's not such a bad thing."

"No." Bobby shook his head, gaze on Lewis' face. "No, you know I don't want that."

"I don't care what you want." Lewis sucked in a huge breath, the air whistling over his teeth. "You can't go on flying."

"For fuck's sake, listen to me." Bobby had to fight to stop his voice from rising. "I've just had the worst reprimand of my life, been humiliated for not doing my job right. A job I want to do, need to do. I fucked up and now they're close to thinking I'm not fit to lead a bomber squadron. I need your support, not you pressuring me as well."

"My support when you could have gone for a desk job?" Anger and desperation were thick in Lewis' voice. "Fuck it. Push pens for a while, just till I get well enough to fly again."

Bobby wiped a hand over his face, dragging at the skin. "That isn't how I want to fight the war," he said simply.

"You..." Lewis' eyes blazed, his fingers tightening until they turned white. He pushed forward, closer into Bobby's space. "Don't you understand? You fucked up because I wasn't with you. We're a lucky pairing—that means we have to stick together."

"Stop saying that, it's stupid. Childish."

"Childish?" Lewis sat back a little. "I'm being childish? I crashed when we were apart. You fucked up when we were apart and still you don't believe your own idea? You fucking thick-skulled idiot, you won't believe the evidence that's right in front of your face." He shook his head, scathing and angry. "Why can't you stay safe, just for a few months?"

"Because..." Again Bobby rubbed at his face, stopping at his mouth as though he could hold the words back. The attempt didn't work. "Because they wouldn't let me. I can't just hop in and out of the war. No one gets that sort of choice. If I push to do something else they might not let me back in when you're well again. I could get stuck somewhere and never get back to an active squadron. I don't want that. I want to fight. I want to be out there doing my part. I don't want to leave things to someone else."

"You'd be damn good at organizing other people, but you won't let yourself do the job. You have to be a fucking hero, killing the bad guy." The scorn was thick in Lewis' tone.

"This is a war—one I believe in. What do you expect me to do?"

"Stay alive so we can fight together."

"I can't, it's not that simple. You know that."

Lewis heaved in a huge breath and held it, as he stared at Bobby critically. "Will you stop for me?"

Bobby looked at him. Everything he'd never even dared to hope for, to think was a possibility. Everything he ever wanted. Everything hanging on his answer.

"No."

Bobby thought that might just be the most important word he'd ever said in his life. The most important and a negative. He'd never imagined that events would turn out this way.

Lewis held himself completely still, his attention fixed on Bobby as the skin on his face turned a motley gray color under the bruises. "I don't mean enough to you."

Lewis wasn't asking a question when he said the words, and that was when Bobby felt the first flare of panic in his belly. "Please, Lewis, please don't say that because it's not true. Don't make it..." He ran out of words as the panic rose like bile, choking his throat.

"Don't make it what?" Lewis' voice was cold, hard. "I'm not the one making anything."

"Please." Bobby deliberately, consciously put every ounce of pleading he could into the word. "Don't make this be the end of us."

"Would you care?"

"Care? I care so much I can hardly breathe."

"But not enough to stop flying." Again the words were a statement.

And that's when he did it, something an hour ago he would have sworn he'd never do because he wasn't made like that. Slipping onto the floor in front of Lewis, on his knees, hands on Lewis' thighs, he pleaded, "I can't stop flying but I'm begging you, please." For a moment the emotion ripped at the air in his lungs and he closed his eyes as he fought to pull himself back together. "Please don't make this the end. My problems aren't important to the world but you are my world. I..." Again he hesitated, wanting desperately to say things right but not knowing how. He'd never even come close to wanting, needing anything like this before, never thought he would.

He honestly hadn't thought he was capable of feeling like this, and he certainly had never thought he'd act this way.

"I've never felt about anyone the way I feel about you." The thought suddenly hit Bobby just how true that statement was and it rocked him in ways he'd never imagined. Off balance, bewildered, disorientated to a degree that left a haze of panic. This wasn't him, wasn't how he acted or felt, but everything was true, real. And he had to make Lewis understand before he lost everything. One chance — he had one chance to say things right. "I love you more than I thought possible."

Still Lewis stared at him but for once Bobby couldn't read his face.

"That doesn't make it right," Lewis said at last.

"It's everything I have to give." Bobby spread his fingers, feeling the warmth of Lewis' skin through the thin cotton of his pajamas. "I give you everything. Please, don't end what we have."

Then there was nothing left to say, nothing left to do but wait for Lewis' answer.

It felt a long time coming. Then Lewis unexpectedly sucked in a huge breath and grabbed Bobby's wrist, his ragged nails digging into the thin flesh covering the veins and tendons on the underside until they broke the skin. "I don't like it." He forced the words through his teeth into Bobby's face. "I don't like it one fucking little bit, but I am not letting you go. Not now, not when I've just found you."

Bobby knew that was the only thing that mattered.

Chapter Six

June 1942

Bobby dragged his feet as he came into his room and threw his cap on the small wooden desk in the corner. He felt tired, beyond exhausted, and not just physically. The war kept going with no sign of an end. The squadron continued to operate, the changing faces of the men in the mess hall testament to the fact that the cost was high. So many men now prisoners of war, injured or, worse still, dead. He knew it was a price that had to be paid but it was a hard one, especially when he was their Squadron Leader.

He sank down on the bed, back against the wall, and huffed to himself as he rubbed his eyes. He needed an early night, but even that wouldn't help with the bone-aching fatigue. For that, he feared, he needed something else. A change from the relentless pressure would be a start.

And someone to share the weight with. Someone other than his current pilot.

Dalip Singh was older than many of the others. He was one of the many Indians in the RAF, one who liked to smoke a pipe and talk cricket. Bobby couldn't abide either of those things, but he recognized a good man when he saw one. A solid pilot and, as the English would say, a decent, all-round chap. Bobby was aware he was picking up more and more English words and phrases every day, but he couldn't seem to stop the process. Wasn't even sure if he wanted to.

No, Dalip wasn't what he needed, it was someone else entirely.

There was a discreet knock on the door and his orderly, Barrett, popped his head round. "Just seen you're back, Sir. I've brought tea." He placed the cup carefully on the desk. "I'm guessing you'll want more cigarettes as well, seeing as you're down to your last couple."

"Thank you." Bobby nodded. "If you can scrounge me another pack I'd be grateful."

"Of course." Barrett hesitated, hand on the doorknob. "How was the journey?" He went on quickly, "The hospital? I mean, will you be needing something a bit stronger than tea?"

A visit to the hospital. Barrett was no fool and he knew what that meant. He'd been posted to the squadron a couple of days before the crash, he'd seen Lewis and Bobby together, around the Mosquito, although he hadn't had cause to speak to them at that point. But he knew about the hospital visits and he also knew Bobby's reaction to them.

The visits were…mixed. Bobby had come to expect that, but the reality was still hard to take. Their tone and content varied wildly, depending on where Lewis was in relation to his skin graft operations. If he was recovering well, the worst behind him for a while, then he'd be calm, thoughtful. There might still be hostility at Bobby's actions, anger even—anger that never went away, sitting like a cloud over the room. But at times like those the anger was restrained, even if the actions weren't understood.

If he'd just been under the surgeon's knife, and the pain and medication levels were high, it was a completely different story. The reality of the situation didn't make Bobby not want to go—he owed Lewis that at the very least—but it did make him wary. An emotional rollercoaster was only the start.

Bobby understood that Barrett had quickly learned to discourage him from any visit if he was about to fly. Discourage as forcefully as he possibly could, suggesting instead that he save them for a quiet, safer time. He knew Barrett had seen how they could rock him but, as a first rate orderly, Barrett protected his Squadron Leader and made sure that no one else noticed.

Lately he'd started asking after Lewis' welfare in general terms. He knew that they were close friends. Bobby hoped he never thought about their relationship any more than that. He was pretty sure that Barrett was smart enough not to do so.

"The visit wasn't so good this time, he's...in a lot of pain." Bobby explained, trying not to let Lewis down.

"Right, sir." Barrett backed out of the room. "I understand. I'll find something, don't you worry."

Why did he feel so disloyal to Lewis when he said something like that? He talked to no one about him but knew—with certainty—that they'd all understand. Burns were so common amongst airmen that everyone knew someone who had been injured that way, knew how painful they were. Knew what the pain could do to a man.

There was another diplomatic knock as Barrett slipped back into the room. "There's a pack of the brand you like," he said, handing over more cigarettes. "And I managed to find a drop of whiskey. I told the man in charge it was in a good cause." He poured Bobby a measure from a quarter-full bottle, putting the bottle down and leaving the glass within easy reach.

Again Bobby nodded his thanks.

"Anything else I can get you, sir?"

"No, thank you. That'll be all for tonight. Goodnight."

"Goodnight then," Barrett said, then added softly, with compassion in his voice, "He'll get better in time."

Bobby pulled his legs up onto the bed, resting his elbows on his knees, as he contemplated the day. The rain was splattering against the window, the noise relentless as it wormed its way inside his mind. Thud, thud, thud. Soft but ever present. A man could go mad with a noise like that constantly in his ear, his head.

A man could go mad trapped in hospital with the persistent, unremitting pain of burns, operations and skin grafts. Sometimes Bobby wondered if Lewis already had. He reached for his glass, draining the contents before topping it up again.

He thought back briefly over the visit, sighed, and gave it more consideration. Today had been a bad time, one of the worst. Lewis had been through another operation. They'd given him morphine but the drug hadn't sent him to sleep by the time Bobby had arrived. He guessed that was the downside of privileged visits at whatever time he could get away. He didn't see Lewis when he was at his best, prepared by the nursing staff. He got reality, in all its gritty, snarling forms. But he owed the reaction his attention and respect, owed Lewis and his pain, his madness. He owed it or it was his duty or something like that, because Lewis had been mad today. Mad with pain and reaction to the drugs. Morphine never went well with him, but nothing else could dull the pain right after an operation. They'd all found that out the hard way.

Today Lewis had been vicious in his anger, calling Bobby appalling names, pouring derisive scorn on his morals, his convictions—hell, his very manhood. Appalling things that, luckily, Lewis at least wouldn't remember when he'd slept the drug off.

The reaction was awful to witness, worse to be the target of, but at least Bobby knew that particular phase would pass. Sadly it wasn't always replaced by something better. Sometimes there was melancholy of the worst sort when Lewis would cry and grieve for all he'd lost, grabbing at Bobby, touching him and holding him in ways he shouldn't. Cry for his mom, his innocence, his childhood.

Cry about how he missed flying.

Missed flying. That was their code for 'I miss you'. Bobby would say, "I miss flying with you" but the words meant the same thing.

And he did. He missed Lewis in a gut-wrenching way that he hadn't anticipated. He'd never missed anyone like this before—not his family nor his friends. Not even his mom. But with Lewis... He shook his head at himself, only too aware of what a stupid fool he was. He missed Lewis like a clichéd arm. He guessed that was only right because he'd never felt like this about anyone else before.

He'd genuinely thought it would be not exactly easy to leave Lewis, but certainly not this hard. Not for so long. Leaving Lewis in the hospital had hurt but he'd thought things would get easier with each successive visit. He had been wrong.

Each time he left it was tough to do, especially so on those days when Lewis was in pain or affected by the drugs. It had only been a few weeks ago when Bobby had arrived to find Lewis huddled at the head of his bed, covers pulled up to his chin, whispering in terror about the unseen monsters under his mattress. How he could hear them scratching in the dark, how they were going to drag him down. How Bobby had to run because they were going to come after him next.

Times like those were awful, when Lewis was most affected by the morphine, most mad. They hurt like a punch to the gut, the shock of seeing him in that state. Lewis wasn't like that—irrational and so very frightened. Bobby longed to be there, to convince him that he was safe. That Bobby would never let the monsters get him. But the medical staff assured him that was perfectly normal and the reaction would wear off quickly.

Bobby prayed that they were right.

He got up, topping up his glass and lighting a cigarette. He needed both. Maybe things would be easier, better, if visits were more predictable. Perhaps all the angry ones together, all the mad ones, all the melancholy, the wistful, the fatalistic. All the sane ones.

He moved to the window, watching the water run down the glass, unable to see anything beyond. He finished his cigarette with the image in his mind of Lewis lying on his belly in the hospital bed, as he'd left him the first time. That day seemed so long ago and Lewis was still there, still hurting.

One more drink and he'd stop. He wouldn't help anyone if he were drunk when he flew in the morning, but... If he could get the amount right, the mellowing effects of the alcohol made the memories come easier. For some reason, tonight, he needed them. However painful, the visits and his recollections of them were a connection to Lewis and he needed that. He sighed, resting his forehead against the windowpane as he thought back.

There were those times when Lewis' anger was overshadowed by apology and despair.

"I caught sight of my back in the mirror yesterday. I should warn you, give you a chance to escape. I look like a monster. Patches of flesh sewn together with black string. Puffy and red, with stuff oozing from the edges. The nurse said it wasn't that bad. When I described what it looked like she laughed at me, said I was seeing things," Lewis had said, eyes wide, face gray. "Maybe that's how my back feels like it should look, rather than what's actually there, I don't know. Whatever the truth, it's only right I warn you. You won't want to get near that and a cockpit is a very crowded space."

Lewis had stared over, a pitiful attempt at a smile on his face before it slid slowly off. "There's me looking like this and you're still flying."

But then there were other times, times when Lewis was in a very different mood.

"I've got to apologize again. Last time you came must have been a doozie of a visit. I can't remember what I said, but I must have been hell from the way everyone looked at me sideways after you'd gone. Shit, I hate morphine. It might work but it messes with my head and the hallucinations are awful. Sorry." Lewis had touched Bobby's knee then, the gesture deliberate, saying so much as his thumb had stroked over and over. "Just... Don't die, I couldn't stand that."

Bobby rubbed at his forehead. He didn't know what was worse. If it was Lewis being so apologetic or the fact that he knew he was mad at times. Knowing that you had been like that, that you would be again? That had to be hard.

By the law of averages the next visit had had to be a better one.

"Today's a good day." Lewis had smiled up from his chair as Bobby had arrived. He'd even offered tea and cake from the trolley an orderly had brought round. "No more morphine, I'm down to drugs I actually like. I went for a walk in the grounds this morning with a guy who has most of his face missing, a Hurricane pilot whose luck ran out. They're trying to build him a new nose—his own one burned. They took skin off his belly, rolled it and attached it to his face. The skin looks a bit like an elephant's trunk. It sure stops me feeling sorry for myself at least."

That was more like the normal Lewis, the one from before, and the thought made Bobby smile back warmer and with more tenderness than perhaps the public space allowed.

Lewis had felt the warmth as well, the need for a little closeness. "I miss flying," he said softly, gesturing to Bobby to pull his seat nearer. Then had come the inevitable, repeated request. "I've been thinking and I know you don't want to hear this but, I'm sorry, I have to say it. You're a fool and you shouldn't be flying. Taking a bit of time out from being in the air wasn't such a big thing to ask. You'd still be fighting, still doing your part in the war, but you'd be safer. I really don't think that was a big deal.

"Instead you leave me here to worry," he went on. "Don't tell me not to, you know that's stupid, there's nothing else to do here except worry and think. The thought is eating me up because it's real, where our luck comes from. Deny it all you want but that's the truth, and I think, deep down, you know it."

He hadn't given Bobby a chance to argue, didn't seem to want to hear his attempt, as though he had a speech rehearsed and he was going to say it. All of it. Bobby thought himself lucky that, for once, the words weren't said with anger.

"The trouble is," Lewis had continued, "I figure we only have so long before our luck runs out and we've pushed it too far already. I'm doing my damnedest to get fit. I make them do the ops as often as they can — even if I do go a bit crazy — but they'll only go so far. They say things have to heal, that the skin grafts or flaps have to grow into the rest of my skin. I'm trying, Bobby. Trying with everything I have but... Don't die before I get back."

But then maybe anger was easier to take than the expression on Lewis' face as he'd said that.

"Think about your options again. If you need to actually fight then take a ground job, man an anti-aircraft gun. You'd be good at that, you know all the tricks pilots pull to evade flak from the ground. You'd shoot them down while they were still thinking how clever they are. Please, think about it, please. I'm begging here, don't fly. We're on borrowed time, we have been for ages."

Maybe visits like that one hurt worst. When Lewis was rational, sounding like he always had — rational, tired and begging. It would be easy to give him that one little thing, to ease his pain by doing what he wanted so badly. But... But what?

Was what Bobby was doing now so important to the war effort?

Yes. The Mosquito squadron made a real difference. That was the simple truth.

Most fit men with decent eyesight and aim could operate an anti-aircraft gun. Bobby made split second decisions out there, in the air, organizing and controlling his planes in ways that meant they were one of the most successful squadrons. He made a difference.

And the cost? Lewis' pain and worry. The ache of missing him so much that, at times, Bobby thought he was going a little insane himself.

Well, there was a war on after all.

Two or three visits ago Lewis had been reflective. He'd never taken his eyes from Bobby's face, as though he were trying to memorize the contours, while he talked on and on like a man desperate for company, for connection. "You know I said nothing ever happens here? I was wrong. Squadron Leader Henderson was supposed to be going home today. Yesterday there was a phone call. He found out he doesn't have a home to go back to. His family—wife and three small children—had been evacuated down near the south coast. They went to a small village, no harm to anyone. A German plane on a raid to Dover caught some damage. To make sure he made the journey back, he dumped the last of his bombs before heading across the Channel. It was a direct hit. They're all dead."

"That's awful," Bobby had tried to say. "But things like that happen in wartime."

"You think we've killed a family like that?" Lewis went on as though he hadn't heard him. "I suppose we have, we must have, more than once. We're always so careful with our bombing—and we've never dumped bombs like that—but it's inevitable. I don't want to think about what could have happened but I should. It's only right. Henderson is on suicide watch."

"Lewis." Bobby had leaned forward, face as close as he dared. "Things happen, it can't be helped, no matter what we—"

"Then this morning the head doctor here got the news that his twin sons were both killed last week. Both of them, in just one week. They were on opposite sides of the war geographically, but they're both dead. That's… I can't think of anything to say how bad that seems right now."

"Neither can I," Bobby admitted. "There aren't words for something like that."

"I'm so glad my family is safe on the other side of the world. I'm even glad that my brother's doing his damnedest to stay as far away from the actual fighting as he possibly can. He's in supply and I don't think he'll leave the States. Can you get much safer than that?"

"No, he'll be okay there. I can't see the fighting reaching America."

"I miss flying so fucking much." Lewis suddenly grabbed at Bobby's wrist, squeezing tight, pressing the bones together as he spoke with startling intensity. "I miss it. Miss the feel of the plane under my hands, the sounds she makes when's she's at the edge, engines screaming, vibrations shuddering through the plywood, miss being in her, where it feels safe, right." He'd stared at Bobby, holding his gaze firm. "Miss just being near her. In that quiet phase, after a raid when I can look at just how beautiful she is. Better than anything I ever dared hope for. I miss flying with you."

Lewis let go then, leaving Bobby feeling the coldness on his skin. "Ever had too much of a metaphor?" Lewis had laughed but the joke wasn't funny, it really wasn't.

Bobby pushed away from the window, turning to look at the empty room. He ran a hand over his face again in a movement full of resignation and frustration. Yes, he was sick of metaphors, sick of being alone, sick of not being what Lewis wanted, needed.

Sick of feeling sorry for himself.

He made himself get ready for bed.

* * * *

Late July 1942

"Please, say there's something hot and decent for dinner tonight?" Bobby asked, as he walked into the mess hall.

"Stew and dumplings, sir," someone called out. "Can't say it's decent but it is good and hot."

"Then that will have to do." Bobby handed over his cap and thick flying jacket, sitting at the end of a long table. A plate piled high with food was placed in front of him.

"I gave you extras, seeing as how hard the last few days have been," the waitress said. "We need to keep your strength up, all of you boys."

Bobby smiled at her. She was a good woman, middle-aged, hearty and plump. Almost a stereotype of herself. A mother figure who wasn't really old enough to be his mother. And she was right because the last few days had been hard.

A hard few days that had ended with too many lost aircraft after a too-long dry spell. Dry in hits, if not weather conditions. Bobby had felt as though they had been flying for nothing. Too long without a decent mission.

He poked at a potato, sliding lumps through the thick, tasty gravy, and thought about what to do next. He had the squadron running as effectively as he could. The men were well motivated, knew their jobs, worked as a team and were damn brave. Wing Commander Stockton still watched him, checked he wasn't slipping again, but he nodded briskly when they met now. Bobby appreciated that. He knew the silent greeting meant that, even if his previous conduct wasn't forgotten, it was most definitely in the past.

For a while, back when Lewis had first crashed and they'd argued in the hospital, Bobby had seriously considered his options. Not just for his sake but also for Lewis'.

He could have pleaded a fear of flying — that happened. Ironically Lewis' accident would've helped. If he had played things properly, made them convincing, they might have transferred him. But who knew if they'd just have stuck a gun in his hand and sent him off as cannon fodder?

And he'd never have flown with Lewis again.

He could have claimed insanity and sat out the next few months in a quiet sanatorium eating bland food that had been blended. An appealing idea at the time but one that didn't make him useful in any way.

And he'd never have flown with Lewis again.

He could have applied to be an advanced instructor. He knew the arguments, that by passing on his skills he'd make more difference than anything he could achieve himself. But the job wasn't fighting and he wanted to fight.

And he'd never have flown with Lewis again.

Take a desk job? Again, no, for the same reasons.

No, there were no options other than be the best Squadron Leader he could, make his the best Mosquito squadron there was. That had been the only way to be useful and win back the respect of the Wing Commander.

He smiled as the waitress slid a bowl full of bread and butter pudding with custard in front of him. Even though the dessert would sit heavy in his stomach he loved this. Starchy and warming—English comfort food at its best.

"Sir!" There was a loud, exasperated bark too close to his ear and he glanced up to see Barrett, with a look on his face to match his tone. "You were miles away there, sir. Thinking about the weather back home? I bet it isn't raining."

"I hope not, at least not all summer, like here. I thought you'd finished for tonight?"

"I had, but I've been looking for you." Barrett pulled an envelope out of his pocket. "I thought you'd want to see this right away, seeing as it's a telegram. I... Well, you know."

Bobby did know. Telegrams most often meant bad news, very bad news. "Thank you," he said, taking the paper cautiously from Barrett's outstretched hand.

The telegram could be something else, though, something from his family maybe. Or did that just mean more bad news? Barrett hovered and Bobby didn't have the heart to send him away. After all, the contents could affect him as well.

The telegram was three sentences long.

Declared fit to fly! Leaving the convalescence home next week when they have a posting organized. See you then.
L

Lewis was fit to fly. He was getting out and he was fit to fly and…

"Good news, sir?" Barrett asked.

"Fucking excellent news." Bobby couldn't stop the huge smile. "My old pilot, Flight Lieutenant Winters, has been declared fit."

"That really is good news, sir. The fact he's well must be a huge relief for you. No more…" He hesitated a moment. "No more difficult visits."

"No. No more difficult visits." Lewis was alive and well and fit to fly.

"So what'll happen now? Will he get light duties? Training or something like that? Or do you think he'll get posted to one of the new areas that need pilots? I hear Mosquitoes are going out to North Africa."

"I don't know," Bobby admitted. Suddenly there was the cold touch of fear in his belly. Just because Lewis was fit didn't mean a damn in relation to Bobby. They weren't linked, joined at the hip or any other ridiculous cliché. There was no reason RAF Command would put them back together. No reason at all.

He pushed away from the table, folding the telegram and shoving it deep in his pocket. "I don't know. I guess I'll have to wait to find out."

"Sir." Barrett stepped out of the way and let Bobby go.

* * * *

It was a long night as Bobby lay awake, staring into the darkness, thinking, just the glowing tip of his cigarette showing periodically. Lewis was so sure that everything was going to be fine, that they'd be put back together immediately and go back to... To what? Bobby wasn't sure, but he assumed that Lewis thought things would be as they had been before.

Could they carry on as they had been? Bobby didn't see why not. They may have only had a handful of visits since Lewis was moved to the convalescence home, but a few weeks apart was nothing. So many people had had to cope with an awful lot longer than that. But the fact that Lewis had been stuck, sitting, doing nothing for months while Bobby had become ever more comfortable and good at his rank might take some getting used to.

The problem was postings. They could both be sent anywhere, any time, because they had no control over orders. Lewis might even get put on another plane, something other than a Mosquito. Bobby considered that for a while. God help the poor soul who had to tell Lewis. Bobby certainly didn't want to be there.

In the end Bobby decided to do the only sensible thing he could. He would talk to the CO, suggesting that there was a good case for putting them back together. That they were a more effective fighting force together than apart.

The next morning Wing Commander Stockton had stared at him but didn't say a word. When Bobby pressed him, the man had simply dismissed him. There was nothing else he could do. He sent Lewis a congratulatory telegram then waited to see what would happen.

Three nights later Barrett knocked on his door, just as Bobby was doing up his tie, ready to go down for dinner.

"Sir, the CO called. He wants to see you in his office asap."

"Now?" Bobby found his cap. "How did he sound? Good mood or not?"

"I'm not sure, sir. But Edna, the typist in his office, said there was a message in from HQ in London. It sounds big. Something is happening."

"Right." Bobby caught his breath, just for a moment, then checked that his uniform was correct one last time in the mirror. "Wish me luck, Barrett, I think I might just need every ounce I can get."

"Good luck, sir. To you and Flight Lieutenant Winters."

Maybe Barrett understood perfectly.

But in reality the waiting wasn't over. The Wing Commander simply handed him some papers and told him he was expected at the Air Ministry the following afternoon.

"But, sir, I'm flying tomorrow," he protested.

"Not now you're not," Davenport said, already looking at other work on his desk. "When Bomber Command calls, you go, it's that simple."

"Yes, sir." Bobby hesitated before leaving. "Any idea what it's about?"

"Davenport." The Wing Commander looked up, kindness as well as respect showing in his eyes. "I couldn't tell you even if I did know. But I've never written you a bad report, never read one about you. You'll soon find out what they have in mind."

The next morning Bobby was standing on a cold, windy train station platform, travel documents and his orders safely tucked in his wallet.

* * * *

"Can you come this way, please?" The young woman in neat RAF uniform and sensible shoes ushered Bobby along numerous darkly paneled corridors to a big, imposing door. She knocked with the backs of her knuckles, opening it so he could pass inside with a quick, "They'll see you now." He smiled and she closed the door behind him.

Inside was a larger room than he'd expect if it was to be a meeting with just a small number of people. There was a big mahogany desk on a raised platform dominating one end, with rows of seats facing the front. What caught his interest, though, were the other people present. There were pilots and navigators from all over the RAF and the Commonwealth. A few he didn't recognize, some he knew personally, others only by reputation. They were all good, very good, if not beyond a simple word like that. These were the best. The best of the best. He felt a thrill to be there with them.

Before he had had much of a chance to greet anyone the door opened and three high ranking officers entered and the room fell silent. "Right, everybody, take a seat and we'll get down to business." Quickly the men all did as they'd been asked. After brief introductions they got started.

"As you know we've begun to make raids deep into Germany, but we haven't been able to cause significant damage, largely because only about a quarter of the bomb loads were delivered on target.

This, when 'on target' is defined as within three miles of the aim point.

"Obviously this isn't good enough. So, after enormous opposition from the Air Chief Marshal Arthur Harris, a decision has been made to set up an elite Pathfinder unit tasked with improving navigation. The job will be to locate and mark targets for the main bombing force to aim at, thereby increasing their accuracy. Harris thinks having an elite will breed rivalry and jealousy, adversely affecting morale in the rest of the RAF. But creating one had to be done and, make no mistake, we've creamed the best from everywhere. A tactic that, understandably, hasn't gone down too well with the Group Commanders.

"Existing partnerships which have excelled will be kept together, if both are agreeable, new ones created where necessary. We need great pilots but this is about navigational skills even more so. We need the best, the most accurate, the bravest. If you need to go around a second or third time to mark the target properly then do so. Wave after wave of bombers will be following your command.

"You are the elite. Eventually you'll get the best planes and equipment but I'll not lie to you, this is going to be a dangerous job. You're going to lead in big numbers of aircraft so, if the enemy stops you, it stops those following you from being effective. It's a dangerous job but a vital one."

He looked at all the men hanging on his every word. "We want you all to be part of the Pathfinders and make a real difference to this war."

Bobby couldn't take his eyes off the men on the platform, couldn't stop the significance of their words from ringing in his head, his chest. He thought all his prayers might just have been answered at once. Or almost all.

It was at that moment that the door opened again and two more men came in. "Sorry we're late, sir," a short, stocky man said in a thick Australian accent. "Train tracks were hit by a bloody great bomb last night, so we had to walk a couple of miles to get past the hole and find another train that was running. Did we miss anything important?"

Bobby glanced over at the door, unable to stop the grin the accent and insanely cheerful tone caused. Then he felt the smile slip off his face like water from a duck's feathers, as his lips rounded into an O shape.

The man following the Australian into the room was Lewis.

Chapter Seven

August 1942

"So." Lewis reached around Bobby to take a cup of tea from the tray that had just been placed on the table. A meaningless movement, uncomplicated and normal for two men who were familiar and easy together after hours squashed in a cockpit. At least that was how the action was intended to be seen, and it worked. As long as no one noticed how he pushed just that little bit closer for a fraction of a second. "Apparently we're the elite, part of the cream of the RAF."

"Well, I am, that's for sure." Bobby couldn't help his big smile, and didn't want to. "Not so sure about you, though. After all, you have been sitting on your butt for the last few months. I'm not convinced you're even fit."

"Me?" Lewis grinned back. "I'll show you just how —"

"Leave the chap alone, Davenport. He's done nothing but sing your praises all the way up to

London. He nearly bored me to death, so it's just as well I've heard such good things about your skills." A large hand descended on Bobby's shoulder and the man Lewis had arrived with turned him round.

"This is Bruce, which is a totally apt name, seeing as he's an Australian. He had to be with a name like that. He's Bruce Patterson," Lewis said. "He's nearly as good a pilot as I am."

"Bloody hell, you—" But Bruce was cut off before he could say any more.

"Right, that's all gentlemen," the Commanding Officer said. "It's good to have you on board. Your new posting details are here ready for you. We'll expect you at the briefing on Monday, 0600 hours. You have time to collect your things from your old postings and you can, of course, arrive at the new base any time over the weekend. We'll see you then."

There was a general standing to attention and salutes then he was gone.

"That means we can all see what the nightlife of London has to offer," Bruce said, rubbing his hands together, a gleam in his eye. "I've already arranged with a couple of the others. You two are going to come along as well, aren't you?"

"Maybe we'll meet you later," Bobby said quickly. "I haven't eaten all day and I know Lewis will need feeding soon. We'd like to catch up as well."

"We're heading to the pubs around Leicester Square—come and find us when you're ready." But Bruce was already moving away, rounding up the others.

"He's going to be a real character," Bobby murmured softly. "We're going to have fun with him around."

They stood side by side, both watching as the other men collected their things and waved goodbye. "Are you really hungry?" Lewis asked.

"Yes, starving."

"So we'll go and find food now."

"I was thinking we might find food after."

"After?" Lewis looked at him properly for the first time in too long.

"Yeah, after."

"After what?"

"After sex. Hopefully? Please?" Bobby gave a knowingly desperate grin.

Lewis' laugh barked out of him, surprising Bobby. "Hell, yes."

"Thank God for that." Bobby snatched up his hat, only just stopping himself from grabbing Lewis' arm as well, as he led the way into the corridor.

"And there I was worried that you'd want to wait, you'd want to make sure I was well enough." Lewis followed after him.

"Fuck that, I can't wait a..." He stopped in mid-stride, turning to face Lewis and lowering his voice. "You are well enough, aren't you?"

"Yes, of course I am, don't be stupid. Although I might not be up to swinging from the chandeliers I can..."

"Once we're in the taxi, make a list of all the things you can do." Bobby pushed Lewis forward again. "I don't care if it's in alphabetical order or sorted by how much effort is needed to do each one. I intend to work through the list any way you write it."

"Shit, you really did miss me." Lewis laughed again. "Sex and then food."

"And then more sex. I haven't touched you in months."

"I haven't touched you either," Lewis said softly, as they walked out of the main door onto the chilly London street. "But I didn't have anything to take my mind off the fact. Just months lying in bed so fucking scared you'd die…"

"I didn't die." Bobby matched his voice to Lewis', moving closer in the gloom of a rainy summer's evening. "And neither did you. Please, can we just enjoy that?" At that moment a light was switched on in a nearby room and, before the blackout curtains could be pulled, the glow fell on Lewis. Bobby saw the real cost of his own stubborn actions. Saw it in the hurt and anguish wrapped in layer upon layer of worry on Lewis' face. Then the look was gone.

"Yeah," Lewis said, a gentle smile warming his eyes. "Let's enjoy being alive. You know somewhere we can go?"

"Better than that, I have somewhere already organized." Bobby moved along the street, looking for a taxi.

"You planned everything."

"Not at all. I didn't know you were going to be here till you walked through the door. No one would tell me anything."

"Now that I can believe." Lewis waved down a passing vehicle. "You should have seen your face. You nearly gave the game away to the whole room with that wide-eyed expression and cheesy grin."

"I—" Bobby stopped, one hand raised as he gazed at Lewis for a moment. He looked so well in his smart new uniform. The old burnt one had been destroyed long ago. Well and healthy and everything Bobby wanted. "You're right, I missed you."

"So stop standing there like an idiot and get into the taxi so you can show me how much."

"I will. I promise you, I will."

* * * *

The hotel was small, down an alleyway off a side street, tucked behind a railway station. Small and gloomy with thick blackout curtains, and a pub next door. The noise of the drinkers and an out-of-tune piano could be heard as they made their way up the stairs to a tiny room at the rear. Bobby's grin was back as he showed Lewis inside. "Aren't we lucky old habits die hard with me? I always get the most secluded room I can."

"Yeah, we're lucky," Lewis said, walking round the bed and already pulling his tie free. "Even luckier that the place is so noisy."

Bobby raised a questioning eyebrow but didn't ask.

"Means we won't disturb anyone when I make you scream." Lewis' voice dropped low and dark while his gaze stayed right where it was, fixed on Bobby's face. "And I intend to make you scream. Scream my name."

"Lewis." The word came out breathy, with a hint of desperation buried deep inside, and Bobby dearly wished he could have kept the sound in. He felt like he was being dragged along by forces he couldn't control and he didn't like that one little bit. Lewis had wanted Bobby to say his name and he'd done just that. But it wasn't Lewis dragging him, making him so needy and vulnerable that was the result of his own emotions. He didn't like the out-of-control, unrestrained intensity of the way he felt, but there wasn't a damn thing he could do about it.

He was caught, hook, line and sinker. But if this was already a done deal he might as well stop fighting and let it all go.

"Yeah?" Lewis dropped his tie on the floor and pulled at the top button on his shirt, the clumsiness of his fingers the only sign that he was anywhere near as off balance as Bobby.

"Let me do that." Bobby moved up close, hands going up to rest on Lewis' shoulders to pause a moment. "There were times when I never thought..."

"Don't," Lewis interrupted. "I can't talk about that, not yet. I need to feel you, touch you, need to..." He bit at his lip for a moment. "Let's just enjoy this, here, now. We can talk later."

"Smart man with a smart plan," Bobby said softly.

He ran his hands forward and down, undoing the buttons of Lewis' jacket before going back up to slip the material from his shoulders. After placing the jacket on the chair with the care it deserved, he turned back to Lewis' shirt. That was a whole different thing. A shirt was a shirt, without all the meaning the uniform held. He worked on the buttons a hell of a lot faster and rougher.

When the shirt hung loose from Lewis' shoulders, Bobby stopped. The cuffs were undone, the tails pulled from Lewis' trousers, all he had to do was take the thing off. He could see skin between the open edges of the fabric, see the edge of a scar at the top. He knew there was worse underneath, a hell of a lot worse. He wanted to see and yet he didn't. He stared up at Lewis and Lewis held his eyes but didn't push him.

Bobby knew this was one thing he had to do in his own time.

He held still for a long moment, lips pressed together, then he moved quickly, pulling the shirt away and dropping it on the floor, until he could see flesh. Not too bad at the front, although there was a puckered mark here, a dip or hole, a line that looked like creased skin. Some still pink with a hint of rawness, the rest white, silvery.

That was the easy bit.

He turned Lewis round, his fingers staying on his waist.

Lewis' back was different and every bit as bad as Bobby had feared. There were large patches of flesh that rippled in unnatural ways, refusing to match the smoothness of the rest of his skin, the look jarring where they met. White, pink, red, traces of purple and blue and all shades in between. Crusted patches, thick ridges, hollows and valleys. The disfigurement stretched from the inner edge of one shoulder blade, across Lewis' back to wrap around his arm. Up over the curve of his shoulder to lick up his neck, thin fingers reaching down, two nearly at the small of his back, another rolling over his spine.

The damage was brutal and relentless. Maybe the scarring could have been better if Lewis hadn't insisted on rushing things, if he hadn't felt pushed by Bobby to do so. His skin would keep healing but the disfigurement would never go away, never stop provoking that sharp intake of breath and horror when it was first seen. His flesh would always be there to remind them both.

But the damage was so much better than it could have been.

"Are you going to breathe? I really think you should," Lewis said over his shoulder. "Or is it that awful?" His face was tight, the small grin pasted on his mouth obviously fake.

"Not awful at all." Bobby's smile was all too real and he suddenly tipped forward, licking a broad stroke right across Lewis' back, over the very worst of the damage. The skin felt strange under his tongue but not shocking or bad. This was still Lewis. He could never be bad.

"Now," he said, suddenly full of a desperate urgency. "I need you now." He pushed and pulled, turning Lewis and maneuvering him until he was flat on his back on the bed. He pressed him down, palm flat in the middle of his chest, the shove harder than he intended. "Fuck, I didn't hurt you, did I?"

"No, course not." Lewis grinned up at him and the look wasn't fake anymore, warmth and excitement flooding his eyes. "I'm not going to break and I love you like this, all needy and frantic."

"I just..." Bobby shook his head, laughing at himself. "I just love you." Then he was working on Lewis' waistband, tugging and dragging at the material as Lewis lifted his hips helpfully. He pulled the rest of Lewis' clothes off with an unintended flourish, throwing them in the corner. Who cared about the sentimentality of a uniform when there was a naked Lewis on the bed? He turned back, ready to laugh at himself, then his breath caught in his chest.

The idea of naked Lewis laid out like a banquet on the bed was one thing—the reality was quite another. His "Oh" of surprise was much louder than he'd hoped.

"Are you okay?" Lewis asked.

Bobby couldn't do anything else but stare for a long moment. "Yeah." He breathed out the word eventually. "But... Your belly? What are those marks?" Across the smooth planes of Lewis' stomach there was a patchwork of shapes, mostly square or rectangular. They had distinct edges and inside the flesh looked pinker, different.

"That's where they took the skin from, to make the grafts for my back." Lewis ran a hand across them, fingertips walking from one side to the other. "They don't hurt but they are a bit more sensitive, I guess because the skin is thinner there."

Bobby caught his tongue between his teeth. "I know you told me but… More sensitive? I'm going to remember that." And still he stood there.

"You can test it out any time you like," Lewis said eventually.

"Yeah." Bobby exhaled nosily. "Just need to look for a bit."

"You take all the time you want." Lewis laughed, soft and so very warm. He closed his eyes, stretching his arms out to the sides, rubbing his palms across the bedspread and letting his legs fall open as he writhed gently and very, very deliberately. His dick was already hard and standing proud.

Bobby looked and looked and… "Oh fuck this." He dove at the bed. It was no accident that he landed with his face in Lewis' groin. He was, after all, an excellent navigator. "I've got to… Now… Right now."

His first taste wasn't tentative or gentle for Lewis' sake, appreciative for his own. He could do that later, would do it. Now he needed all he could get.

He lunged at Lewis' cock sucking in as much as would fit, forcing his head down so that the cockhead scraped across the top of his mouth, hitting his throat much too hard. But he wasn't going to stop. He was never going to stop.

He pushed his arms under Lewis' thighs, scooping them up and pulling them around himself so he was buried as deep as he could get, and sucked hard. Lewis had no choice but to buck up, his hips pushing farther into Bobby's face as he scrabbled for purchase on the covers. Bobby sucked and sucked again, no finesse or style but all his feelings laid out as bare as the man on the bed.

Lewis threw his head back, his chest heaving as he panted, as he groaned. The sound was deep, powerful and all man.

The reaction made Bobby ache for more. He sucked again, his nose touching pubic hair, and gripped Lewis' thighs tighter, pulling them against his face.

Pressing his tongue to the underside, he caught his lips over his teeth and raked his way back up, filling his senses with the taste, the smell. He tried to suckle at the tip, knowing how Lewis loved that, but it wasn't enough. Nothing would ever be enough. Without thinking he forced his way back down as hard and fast as he could, the circle of his lips as tight as he could make them.

Lewis came with his back inches off the bed, his neck arched painfully, his fingers twisted in the covers and a cry on his lips. Bobby let the warm liquid flood his mouth, swallowing most, letting the rest ride over his lips to slide down his chin and Lewis' cock.

Eventually, when Lewis started to stroke his head, Bobby made himself pull off but he wasn't going far. He'd be back for more soon but nothing would ever be enough. He rested his cheek on Lewis' thigh, conscious of the marks on his belly, and sighed. Lewis' hand turned ever more gentle as he ran his fingers through the strands of Bobby's hair, tangling in deep.

Bobby didn't want to move, not ever.

The room was silent except for the distant sounds from the pub next door and Lewis' breathing as the panting slowly calmed. After a long while Lewis spoke, his tone soft. "How's your throat? I'll bet it's sore."

"It'll be all right," Bobby said, but his voice sounded wrecked. He felt a little wrecked as well.

Bobby sensed Lewis' answering smile in the tightening of his thigh muscles.

"You're going to have fun explaining that when we get to the airfield." Lewis started stroking again. "But we'll think of something. Together we'll think of something good."

Bobby nodded, pressing his nose into the delicate flesh of Lewis' inner thigh.

"Hey," Lewis said, after another couple of minutes. "No going to sleep down there, it's my turn now."

Bobby tipped his head back and grinned up. "I have no intention of going to sleep. I have lots more things planned."

"I like the sound of that." Lewis tried to pull him up. "You could start by taking your clothes off. The material's rough and the buttons are digging in."

Heaving himself up onto his hands, Bobby looked down between their bodies. "Call me a pervert but I like the contrast of you stark bollock naked and I've only taken my hat off. That's... That's really damn hot."

"Pervert." Lewis grinned. "Great big freaking pervert that I've missed so fucking much the pain was like having both my arms and a leg cut off."

"Three limbs? That's impressive, but you kept a leg." Bobby inched his way up until his hands were either side of Lewis' head. He let his hips fall, rubbing the coarse uniform material over Lewis' very naked skin.

"That one was going atrophied and withered. It was about to— Would you take your clothes off? Now, right now, before I'm forced to do it for you or beat you to death."

"You could strip me with your teeth and— Oh fuck that, it'd take too long. Kiss me and I will."

"You didn't even have to ask." Lewis caught a hand round Bobby's neck pulling him down the last few inches. The kiss was sweet, warm and gentle with so much feeling running through it that Bobby thought he might just drown. But what a way to go. He couldn't think of any way better. "You taste of me." Lewis smiled.

"As I should. I love you," Bobby whispered, as he tilted his head, their noses bumping and brushing until they lined up again. He licked across Lewis' lips, purposefully dragging his tongue, searching out as much contact as he could find.

"I love you more," Lewis huffed into his mouth, both hands buried deep in Bobby's hair, refusing to let him move an inch away.

"I'm not arguing, I know the truth." Bobby exhaled hard, his hips undulating, knowing the reaction he was causing. "You're right about one thing. I do need to get naked right now." But he was reluctant to leave Lewis' mouth, faltering as he simultaneously tried to get off the bed and kiss Lewis farther, deeper, wetter. More.

"Move." Lewis pushed at his shoulders. "Please."

"Please?"

"Yeah, I want." It was Lewis' turn to breathe out hard. "I want more."

Bobby scrambled backward, discarding his clothes as he went, his normal respect and attention to detail with his uniform blown away. Then he was naked, hands hanging by his sides as he hesitated for a completely different reason.

"What do you want?" Again he blew out a breath, tongue stroking across his bottom lip. "What can I do to make you feel good?"

"Whatever. As long as I get you I don't care," Lewis said.

"But... I want..."

"What do you want, Bobby? Tell me, what do you want?"

Bobby unknowingly closed his eyes for a moment and the words slipped over his lips without any conscious thought. "I want to keep you." And there it was, everything Bobby had struggled to admit to himself, laid out, open and exposed, more naked than his body could ever be. All for Lewis to see. He had principles, ideals that he would fight for, willingly give his life for, and he would never give those up. But this here, now, Lewis. This was what he wanted deep down in his bones, his soul.

"Don't you get it, you idiot?" Lewis smiled at him with warm affection. "That's not something you have to fight for, you already have me. I made the decision ages ago, fool. You get to keep me forever."

Bobby didn't know what to say, what to think, how to breathe. He pitched forward, landing on the bed and Lewis pulled him up between his legs, big hands cradling his face until he had no choice but to feel safe.

"Take, take all you want," Lewis said. "I'm here."

"I..." Bobby tried to speak, but his voice wasn't steady or sure, wasn't there.

"I know." Lewis kissed him again, tongue licking in deep, controlling and calming. "I know how you feel. How it's all so much you think you can't cope but you can, because I'm here with you." He suddenly flashed a grin so full of lust and humor that at any other time

Bobby would have been asking why. "Now we're going to seal the deal with a fuck."

"A fuck?" Bobby tried to smile back. He was so grateful he thought he might just come apart.

"Yeah, it seems...appropriate." Lewis pulled his knees open and back. "What are you waiting for?"

"You want me to fuck you?"

"Of course I do." Lewis pushed a hand down between them, gripping Bobby's cock and stroking with a firm, sure hand. "Now would be nice."

"Now." Bobby grinned, his lips pressed against Lewis', insanely happy. He hooked an arm under Lewis' leg, lifting it and letting his cock slide against Lewis as he kissed him again. He reached out, hand searching, but Lewis came to the rescue again, pressing the grease he'd brought with him into Bobby's palm.

They didn't need much in the way of preparation, the necessities well practiced, preferences well established. Then Bobby was pressing in, his bottom lip caught between his teeth, his eyes closed, until he was all the way inside. Then he paused, the moment both constricting his breathing and capturing his sensations. This was so much more than sex, so very, very much more.

"Move," Lewis whispered, fingers pressing into Bobby's shoulders, his biceps. But Bobby couldn't, not yet, not until Lewis added, "I need you to."

If Lewis needed, Bobby would provide.

Instinctively he dragged his hips back, nowhere near ready to pull out completely, before thrusting back in. He rested his forearms by Lewis' head so he could stroke his fingers through his hair, tangling them in. Events didn't last long, nothing like as long as Bobby would have liked. All too soon he was coming with a yell on his lips and the threat of tears pushed down as deep as he could hide them. All too soon.

As he eased his way down to rest on top of Lewis he reached down between them to Lewis' cock. It was still hard. "I'm sorry, that wasn't fair. I should have —"

"Shhh," Lewis stopped him with soft fingers to his lips. "You shouldn't have done anything."

"But I —"

"If you hadn't been so desperate, so needy, so fucking perfectly out of control, you would have realized I was holding back, stopping myself from coming."

"You stopped yourself? Why?" Bobby looked down, eyes wide and round.

"Because I need to fuck you," Lewis said quite deliberately. "I need to, to make sure. To make us forever."

Bobby felt his eyes widen impossibly as his breath caught. "How do you want me?"

"Any way, doesn't matter, as long as I can get deep."

Bobby could feel the heat pulsing behind the skin on his face as he, very consciously, closed his mouth. He rolled over, half on his belly, half on his side, and pulled his top knee up to his chest. Best way he knew to get Lewis as deep as possible.

Lewis stroked over Bobby's hip in appreciation, kissing his shoulder as he got them both ready and pushed in. "I want slow and steady," he said, open mouth hot and damp against Bobby's flesh. "I want to savor and — Shit." He groaned as the pace picked up, both their bodies dictating the speed.

Bobby reached back, pulling him closer, fingers spread as wide as he could get them. "It's okay."

"Of course it is," Lewis managed to say between thrusts that pushed Bobby forward, rolling him farther until Lewis was spread out over him. "We have time."

Bobby pressed back, feeling himself safe and surrounded. He'd wanted this for so long, missed the feeling so badly it was in danger of overwhelming him. He could either fight how he felt, and keep some semblance of his rational self, or let go and revel in the moment.

Lewis reached round, forcing his hand between Bobby and the bed to hold him tighter. "I wanted to see your face but..." He stroked in again, and again, his breath stuttering as he did so. "I can hear your reaction, feel it under my hand, through my cock."

The idea of that was too vivid, too intense for Bobby to think about. He gave in to everything, pushing back as hard as he could, letting his orgasm flood over him until he could taste it. Every nerve ending was firing, every sensation heightened and he could feel Lewis' dick pulsing as he came, feel the hot liquid inside him.

Lewis gave a last, futile, thrust, groaning as he rocked his hips, and buried his nose in the back of Bobby's neck, his arms squeezing one last time. "Missed you so much..." He stopped, breathing deeply, then started to ease back out, but Bobby caught him by the hip again, holding him in place.

"Tell me," Bobby asked, knowing there was more Lewis needed to say.

"There were times..." Lewis started slowly, licking at his lips as he seemed to hesitate for a moment. "Times when I couldn't remember how you smelled. The disinfectant and burnt flesh smell of the hospital got in my nose, my mouth. The place tasted of sickness, of death, and I couldn't find your smell anymore." He rubbed his face across Bobby's skin, his mouth open, his tongue out. "I needed to taste you, to smell you, to feel you."

Bobby rolled back, just enough to ease Lewis off him and out. He turned inside the arm that was still draped over him, until they were face to face and he looked at Lewis. Really studied him. He saw the hurt that still lay at the back of his eyes but also the easing of the tension in his face.

He'd made a start. He'd work on the rest.

Closing the small gap, he kissed Lewis, slow and deep. He cupped Lewis' face. He kept going, unable to stop as he thoroughly re-explored his mouth, missing nothing as he took his time. "Do you know how I taste now?" he asked, eventually.

"Yeah." Lewis practically sighed, his eyes hazy.

"Good, I still need to taste you."

"Haven't you already done that?"

"A bit, mostly parts I already knew." Bobby's smile was warm but it soon fell, leaving behind nothing but seriousness. "But there are new parts of you. I want to taste them as well."

It was Lewis' turn to stare with wide eyes.

"Roll over," Bobby said gently, his hands guiding. For a moment Lewis hesitated, then he complied, lying on his belly as Bobby settled him.

Bobby rested a palm on the small of Lewis' back, sitting up as he did so. Lewis folded his hands under his face, twisting his neck so he could watch Bobby. "You don't—"

"Shut up." Bobby stopped him, making circles with his hand on Lewis' skin. "I need to do this." He sat back and simply looked for a long while. He'd seen the damage earlier, but that was through a thick fog of lust and need. He'd seen and tasted but didn't know this new flesh, and he wanted to. He wanted to know all of Lewis.

He ran his fingertips very softly up over the worst of the disfigurement to Lewis' shoulder. The skin was rough, bumpy, with edges and ridges that shouldn't have been there. The worst would heal, become healthier than now, smoothing out and losing the disturbing coloring. But it would always be there. These were deep scars that covered too much damage.

They would always be there. Which meant that Bobby would live with them and love them.

He used both hands to stroke across the flesh, letting his fingertips wander until the texture became recognizable, no longer shocking, until everything was familiar. This would be a part of his life just as much as Lewis would be.

"You know that tickles, don't you?" Lewis said softly.

"Tough. Suck it up like a man." The smile was thick in Bobby's voice as he leaned forward, leaving his first kiss on Lewis' damaged shoulder, taking his first real taste.

Moving slowly, carefully, methodical to the last detail, he made sure he covered every inch, every molecule of new skin with his mouth and his tongue. Stopping nowhere, missing nothing. Out to each farthest edge to feel where the scarring started, tracing around the edges so he would know it all. He had to know each line, every transition. Dividing the whole so he could map every section, not missing a fragment.

"It's..." Lewis' voice was breathy, wobbling in ways it never normally did.

"What?" Bobby lifted his head for a moment. "Does your back hurt?"

"No. No, it doesn't hurt. It feels… I don't know. In some places I can barely feel you, like there's clothing in the way. In others the sensation is stronger, more intense."

"I have to learn this, all of it," Bobby said, bending his head back to his task, taking his time. "I want to know every part. Where you feel most sensitive, what feels best. Everything."

"And you will," Lewis said eventually. "But it's changing as it heals. It feels different, plus what I can feel changes."

"I want to know all of that. I want to be part of the healing process." Bobby licked a wide stripe right up through the heart of the damage, then another and another and another.

"Stop." Lewis laughed, pushing Bobby away so he could roll over. "You're going to be here for everything but right now stop. You've made it all tingly and wet."

"Too much?" Bobby kissed the patches on Lewis' belly but this he knew — his flesh might look different, feel different to Lewis, but it was the same tight skin over hard muscle Bobby had known before. He gave each a last lick then stretched out next to Lewis.

"The tingly I can take, the wet is just…wet."

"And you can't take wet? You've forgotten we're in England. The weather is always wet here."

"I know. I haven't forgotten anything." Lewis' expression suddenly turned serious. He ran a finger down Bobby's nose, studying him. "You haven't had enough sun, you've gone pale and your freckles are standing out more than ever. I…" He drew in a deep breath, letting it out slowly. "I haven't forgotten a damn moment."

"Do we have to talk about it now?" Bobby asked, no hint of incrimination or frustration in his voice. "Can't we just enjoy what we have?"

"Maybe."

"No, that's not going to work, is it?" Bobby didn't wait for an answer. "Before we can be happy I have to let you say what you need to, to get it out there. Otherwise it'll be like a monster constantly sitting in the corner of the room. I know that."

"I'm not sure if you're right," Lewis admitted after too long a time. "When things are said, they can't be taken back."

Bobby gave a small hint of a smile, there and gone in a moment. "The monster will only grow if we ignore it. Get so big it'll crush us." He smiled again. He knew it was tinged with regret but it was bigger "It'll be better if we talk now. But you have to do it right." He angled his head, watching Lewis closely. "Don't vet your words—say what you mean, from the heart. I know you love me."

"And I know you love me." Lewis stopped, fingers tapping against the bed, eyes still fixed on Bobby. "Which is why I couldn't, and still can't, understand why you wouldn't do that one thing for me." Bobby went to speak but Lewis didn't seem ready for that, not yet. He put a fingertip on Bobby's lips. "You told me to say it from the heart—now you have to let me." He lifted his hand away, ghosting over Bobby's face. "I know you thought I was crazy and maybe I was, but I was also right. Even if I wasn't, I believed it. Why couldn't you go along with that? Why couldn't you have stopped flying?"

"Because this war matters," Bobby started but again Lewis wasn't finished.

"Yeah, I know it matters. I may be like a kid around planes but I'm not stupid. You could have done something different in those months I was out of action, taken the desk job, trained the new kids. Fuck it, Bobby, if you didn't believe me you could at least have humored me." Lewis' voice had changed as he spoke—the volume stayed low, but now it was laced with anger.

Bobby adjusted himself on the bed, accepting the depth of feeling aimed at him. "I knew you'd got things all mixed up, back in the hospital, that you'd got things out of proportion but..."

"Out of proportion?" Lewis' eyes widened, the skin across his cheekbones pulling tight. "You have no idea what you're talking about."

Bobby wiped at his face, desperate for a cigarette but knowing he couldn't move to get one. "So tell me."

"Things were so..." Lewis seemed to fight to find the right words. "So black. All I had was pain, knowing there was more to come, that and madness. Yeah, I knew the drugs made me crazy. I heard you talking to the doctors but I knew anyway, what the drugs and the pain did to me. They clouded my mind so bad I didn't know which way was right, like if you spin your plane enough you don't know if the ground is below or above you. All I had was pain and the knowledge there was more coming and it would send me crazy again and again. There was only one spark of light and that was you, us. I'd been looking for you for years, and then there you were, and I had you, and..." He ran a fast hand back through his hair, his breathing coming ragged and harsh. He inhaled hard before blowing the air out slowly.

"I had you and you kept saying I was what you wanted but you were throwing what we have away, risking everything. I know you have your principles, that they make you who you are, and I admire that in you. Damn it, I'm proud of you for them, but you were wasting everything we had. A few months was all I was asking—they'd have let you, you could have found a way. But no. Whether you believed me or not, either way, I didn't matter enough for you to give me those few months."

Bobby stared at Lewis in astonishment. "I didn't know I was looking," Bobby said, and his voice didn't sound like his own. He couldn't stop the tremor running through the words, couldn't stop his hand shaking when he lifted it to rub over his mouth.

"Didn't know you were looking?"

"You said you were looking for me—well, I wasn't looking for you. People like me don't get someone. All we get are one-night stands, if we're lucky. Dirty, sordid acts hidden in dirty, sordid places. They told me enough times in church, school, at home. All the men out drinking, laughing about our kind. We don't get to be happy." Bobby hadn't meant to say any of that, hadn't even acknowledged to himself how he felt. But Lewis had triggered something and now he couldn't stop.

"You believed them? Believed we couldn't be happy together?" Lewis' confusion turned to concern.

"I believed we couldn't be together at all, that people like us never found anyone. That there was no chance of someone smart and decent and good, not for me. There was no chance so I never even looked for you. All those years on my own and I never even looked." Even to Bobby's ears his voice sounded stretched thin to the point of almost breaking, the tremor opaque, real. He pleaded silently with Lewis to understand, as he tried to apologize for the years before they'd met.

"My mom wanted me to make her proud. She used to straighten my clothes before I went to school and say it every day, 'Make me proud'. When my brother brought home his rich girlfriend my mom patted my shoulder and told me there was more than one way to make her proud." He closed his eyes, just for a moment, trying to collect himself. "She may not always agree with my politics but she admires my conviction. That I don't just talk, I'll fight for what I believe in."

"So you found another way to make your mom proud of you. Now be proud of yourself."

"I'm a dirty, stinking queer," Bobby said, and they'd both heard that line enough times to know just how the words hurt.

"No, you're a brave and amazing man. You just have to accept that. Accept that and everything else."

"I-I-I..." Bobby said, feeling his face infusing with color before immediately draining. "I love you so much and I didn't think that was even possible. I didn't know how to love and... I sat in the hospital looking at you and I got scared, worse than anything I've ever felt flying. So fucking scared of how you made me feel. You were hurting, I could have lost you and I was hit with all these thoughts I couldn't cope with. I felt out of control and that left me reeling, vulnerable, and I got shit scared."

He rolled onto his back, both hands at his face now, rubbing hard, before he turned back. "You were asking me to think about who I am, what's important to me. Well, I'd built up this idea of myself. I'm queer and alone but a good fighter, one who isn't afraid to stand up for what he believes in. Then you come along and I don't even recognize myself. All I knew was you made me happy but I wasn't allowed to be happy, not for long. What did it matter anyway, if I was happy or not? There's a war on and I'm not important. So I was certain something was going to happen and I'd lose you and everything would go back to how it was before, being alone. Only now I'd know what I'd lost, what I'd never have again. It seemed simple, get everything over with, die doing something worthwhile that could make a difference and —"

"You fucking stupid asshole." Lewis caught hold of Bobby's face, his hands bracketing the sides, fixing him in place, grounding him. "How did somebody so smart get to be so stupid? I'm not going to die because you love me, because you're happy. You think Hugo or any of the others died because someone loved them? No, and we're no different. We're just an insignificant couple in a world that shouldn't care about us. If I die it'll be because of the war, because it's my turn." He snorted, raising a rueful eyebrow. "Or because I'm executed for killing you for being an asshole. At least that way we'd both be dead." Lewis shook his head. "I didn't know you felt like that. You should have told me." He stroked Bobby's cheek with his thumb, shaking his head again.

Bobby felt as though, if he took his gaze away from Lewis, one of them might just stop existing.

"Are you proud of me?" Lewis questioned.

"Of course I am. How can you ask that?"

Lewis didn't answer the question, putting one of his own. "Are you proud of us? Proud of what we are when we're alone together and —"

"You don't have to qualify it." Bobby interrupted. "I'm proud of us."

"Good." Lewis tipped his head in acknowledgment. "But if you're proud of us and proud of me with all my madness..." He raised an eyebrow and Bobby nodded, agreeing. "Then respect my madness. We're a lucky pairing, we need to stick together, and you have to accept that. You should have stopped flying because I asked you to. I'm not sure I'll forget what you did or ever totally forgive you, but it's done now, it's over." He said the words simply, softly, with no hint of blame or anger.

"But we haven't made it this far because we're a lucky pairing," Bobby said, and he could see the surprise on Lewis' face.

"So why then? Is this another one of your crazy ideas that'll eat away at me?"

"Not crazy. Probably stupid, but I'd like it to be true." Bobby exhaled slowly, concentrating on the breath as he thought. He rolled onto his belly closer to Lewis, a hand propping up his chin. "We made it because…" He stopped, taking another noisy breath. "My mom's a very religious woman—the whole family is. She made the church's views on people like us very clear—never anything directly about me, but always so I could hear. I knew the words of the preachers. But, I think, just maybe God doesn't agree, maybe He wanted a little bit of good." He looked up at Lewis, knowing there was hope and a smudge of embarrassment showing in his eyes. "God made us a spot of happiness in his world, even if we're the only ones who know what He did." He laughed then, more scorn than happiness in the sound. "Or maybe it just wasn't our turn to die. That date is next week or next year. Perhaps I should believe in fate more than anything else."

"You're as mad as I am and that makes me love you even more." Lewis smiled, pushing a strand of hair off Bobby's forehead. "I like the idea, though, that God wanted a little bit of light in a dark world. I know He'd see what we have as a good thing."

Bobby ducked his head. "I hope so."

"I know so." Lewis stroked over the skin of Bobby's naked shoulder. "But that opens up another possibility – if He really is on our side we might just stay alive till the end of the war."

"Now you're pushing things." Bobby smiled. "I don't think it's worth thinking about that."

"I do."

"Come on, being a Pathfinder is about as dangerous as life gets in the RAF. We'll be leading in waves of bombers, going low to mark the target accurately. If they can take us out, the raid won't be worth half as much. The whole of the Luftwaffe is going to be after us – there's not much chance of us making it to the end of the war."

"But we might."

"There's no point thinking about that, not now."

"I want to," Lewis said very quietly, his fingers stilling. "I want something to think about, to imagine. The other men have lives to go back to, wives and girlfriends. I don't want to go back, not without you."

The thought hit Bobby then, like fire at the back of his throat. He didn't want to go back either, not to his old life. Not to any life without Lewis. "Neither do I."

"So what else is there? Give me a fantasy, a dream. Give me something to hang onto when times are bad."

"I don't know…" Bobby considered, going through ideas, possibilities. "There has to be somewhere in the world that doesn't care what we are, that will let us live in peace. I don't know – the Far East, India, somewhere warm and relaxed. Maybe a tiny island in the Pacific, somewhere where a plane will make a difference to their lives. We'll start a little business running goods and people around, we'll be a taxi in the air."

"We could island hop." Lewis smiled, his fingers moving again. "Maybe get a seaplane."

"Maybe." Bobby grinned back at him. "I don't care where as long as we can stay together."

"We'll find our place."

"Is that a fantasy worth hanging onto?" Bobby asked softly.

"Nope, that's beyond a fantasy, that's a possibility. That'll do me just fine."

"Me too." Bobby admitted.

"Are you happy now?" Lewis asked.

"Of course I am."

"No, think about the question properly," Lewis said, running strands of Bobby's hair through his fingers again. "Right now, are you happy?"

"Look at what I've got." He waved a hand absently, indicating the bed and themselves. "You and me, no monster hiding in the corner and the knowledge that we have tomorrow. What's not to be happy about? We're even RAF elite now."

Lewis lay back, one hand under his head. For once, when he looked at Bobby, it wasn't with lust. This time it was with deep-rooted affection and pride showing on his face. "So you're happy we've got this job, happy now you're doing something important?"

Bobby stopped and thought about things carefully. "Yes," he said honestly. "It matters to me that I do a job that's worthwhile. But you've made me realize that you matter. We matter. I want this but I want you with me while I do it even more. That's a huge thing for me, admitting that, not only to myself but also to you. You do know that, don't you?"

"Yeah, I know." Lewis reached over, resting a hand on Bobby's shoulder. "You know how I know? Because you let me in and that's an even bigger thing for you. Fighting this war comes first but, I think, I hope, I'm high up on the list after that."

Bobby watched him for a long moment, his face as serious. "That's what I'm trying to tell you," he said at last. "You're next on the list. Hell, you're the most important thing apart from the war."

"Good thing you have me then, isn't it? Because I'm not going anywhere." Lewis' eyes were sparkling, his smile as wide as the whole of Texas.

"Are you happy as well? Really happy?" Bobby just had to ask.

"Sure I am, you know that. Even better now I have a hazy image of our future. It doesn't matter if we're shot down next week. I mean, hell, I want to make it through this but if we don't, at least we won't make it together and…" Lewis suddenly stopped, his face clouding. "Hey, what type of planes do Pathfinders use?"

"They're going to use all sorts but we've got…" Bobby paused, just for a bit of dramatic effect. "Mosquitoes, you idiot." he laughed. "We're flying a Mosquito."

"Really? Then that's just about perfect." Lewis shrugged, so simple, so casual. "Except for us winning the war, of course."

Chapter Eight

January 1945, Petwood Hotel, near the RAF Base, Lincolnshire

Bobby pulled back the floral curtain and stared out of the window. He couldn't quite believe it—January 1945 and they were still alive. Surely the war couldn't last much longer? Maybe Lewis was right, maybe they would both make it to the end intact if they stayed together. They'd made it this far so who knew?

But thinking something like that, let alone saying it out loud, felt like tempting fate. He frowned at his reflection in the glass and tried to enjoy the beautiful gardens outside instead.

"You're doing it again," Lewis said, settling back in his chair and stretching his legs out in front of him whilst trying to balance a tea cup on his chest. "I can hear you from here, you're worrying again."

Bobby made a conscious effort to straighten his spine and push shoulders back before turning round. "It's my job to worry, that's what I'm paid to do."

Lewis just grinned at him and Bobby had to give in to the urge to smile back. The last two and a half years had changed Lewis, aged him in many ways. His face had more lines and there was a shadow at the back of his eyes caused by too much destruction and too many lost comrades. But he still had his thick, uncontrollable hair, and gloriously long legs. He'd also become increasing adept at reading Bobby. Much to Bobby's annoyance.

"You'd have even more to worry about if you'd taken the Wing Commander promotion this time. You'd enjoy that, and you'd only have to do it for a short period before they made you Group Captain, with all the worry that would entail."

"I told you, I'm not sitting behind a desk…"

"…sending other men into danger when you're safe back here pushing papers around," Lewis finished his sentence for him. "Yes, I know. I've heard that speech so many times I can recite it." Lewis got up and came over to stand next to him.

"You do understand, don't you?" Bobby said quietly.

"Of course I do." Lewis stroked over Bobby's cheek then tucked a nonexistent strand of hair behind his ear. "Even though I think you'd make a great Wing Commander, and I'd love to know you were safe, I can't say I'm disappointed. It would have meant that I'd have to get a new navigator and I've only just broken you in to the way I like." He grinned again but Bobby knew how he really felt.

"You could be a Wing Commander as well, if you wanted."

"And give up flying? Like that's going to happen."

"You could at least be a Squadron Leader." Bobby put the idea out there yet again, although he was pretty sure of Lewis' reaction.

"And give up flying with you? Don't be an ass."

"But you'd be good."

"So would you as Wing Commander, but neither of us is going to do it, so forget it."

"It means that we can't stay here, though," Bobby said softly.

"And won't you love worrying about the men when we move on. You do know there are other Squadron Leaders that are almost as good as you?"

"Almost," Bobby said, and grinned. "But we're giving up a lot of other things as well." He glanced around the room, knowing that Lewis would understand.

They had been lucky with their posting for the last fourteen months. The RAF base didn't have enough accommodation for the whole squadron so the officers were billeted at the nearby Petwood Hotel. Not only did it boast lovely grounds but the house also had paneled rooms and high ceilings, which provided a wonderful haven, and the mess had hosted more than a few parties.

As Squadron Leader, Bobby had been given his choice of room. Unsurprisingly he'd gone not for the grandest but for a small, and much more isolated, room up in the attic. Lewis didn't stay overnight but, if pilot and navigator needed to discuss things post or pre operation, in private, no one was going to question it. Their policy of letting everyone pretend they didn't know was working well. Their ability at their jobs, and the fierce loyalty and respect the men held for their leader, didn't hurt either.

Now they would be losing the comfort and privacy as they were due to be reassigned. It also meant a new squadron, something neither wanted. The thought must have registered on Bobby's face because Lewis patted his arm. "Go on, go and find out where they're sending us. I'm praying it's Kent, not Scotland. I swear, up there it starts raining the day I arrive and doesn't stop until I leave. The place hates me."

"It doesn't—" Bobby started to say but thought better of it. It did rain whenever Lewis was in Scotland. The one time he'd had to go back to London for training, the sun had come out the whole time he was away. He'd refused to believe their stories when he got back, until he saw the sunburn on the top of the bridge of Bobby's nose. "I'll put in a good word for Kent."

"Make it heartfelt," Lewis said, then kissed him quickly. "You must have some influence, being one of the best Master Bombers in the RAF."

"I don't think it works like that." Bobby smiled ruefully. Over a year before, after he'd refused promotion yet again, Bobby had been made one of the new Master Bombers, a role usually taken by a pilot. The 'single mind' method of controlling attacks had proven to be more effective on the Dam Busters raid and was now widely employed. It was Bobby's job to make sure that the target markers had been dropped in the right place before calling in and organizing the waves of the main bombing force. Sometimes that could be more than six hundred aircraft so they had to fly low to check, reset the indicators if necessary, and check again.

Bobby loved the work and also loved knowing he was doing a vital job, one that few others could do.

Lewis just adored having an excuse to fly that low. "Do your best because I'll go rusty in the rain. And don't stay in London too long." He shrugged and kissed Bobby again. "Fuck knows why, but I'll miss you."

Bobby thought about that on the long train ride down to London. He thought about the kiss, full of love but easy and comfortable, as they had become together. They were sure in how they felt and their commitment to each other. It was more than Bobby had ever thought possible and it was theirs.

He'd miss Lewis just as much.

But it would only be for one night and the war wasn't over yet. He was ready for a new challenge.

* * * *

Bobby hadn't been to London for over six months and had forgotten how big it was. As he caught his first bus for the journey across the city he tried to catalog the damage. Single houses were missing in some places, whole streets reduced to rubble in others. The bombing had never stopped and now there was a new weapon being launched at the city. Since the D Day landings at Normandy in June 1944, V1 flying bombs had been hitting London. Now came the silent terror of the V2 rocket. The first people knew about it was when it exploded.

But still people got on with daily life — women with their neat hair and baskets, going shopping and queuing for their rations. The few children that were left in the city searching for shrapnel. Men in all different types of uniform either striding out purposefully or heading toward the pubs. Hitler might have done all he could to destroy London but the city still lived and would continue to do so.

Bobby got off the bus and, skirting round a heavily pregnant woman with a sailor on one arm and a soldier on the other, headed across the road. He was due to meet Bruce Patterson, and they would travel on to RAF Command together, but he couldn't see the man anywhere. Maybe Bruce had been forced to change his plans — it was a common enough occurrence. Bobby stood in line at another bus stop, outside a Woolworth's store, and looked in through the window. There wasn't much on sale but two ample-bosomed ladies appeared to be arguing over balls of brown wool. Bobby couldn't help smiling to himself — human nature never changed.

It was at that moment that time seemed to stop for a fraction of a second as the air stood still.

It felt like the world held its breath for a moment then a thunderous noise came from everywhere at once. The wave of sound hit Bobby smack in the middle of his chest, making his whole body shake and his ears ring.

A colossal flash of intensely, horrendously bright light blinded him. His face was suddenly incredibly hot, the fine hairs sizzled away in an instant, and he was in the air, flying, unable to tell the direction of the ground.

Then all he could sense was pressure, pressure, pressure. Pushing him. Dragging at the skin on his face, his clothes, squeezing the breath from his body.

Pain.

Pressure, pressure and more pressure.

The relief of darkness.

He could only have been unconscious for a short while because, when he came round, dust was still settling on his face and the air was thick with it. His first irrational thought was that he could now say he'd experienced the infamous V2 rocket for himself.

He tried to organize his mind and assess his body. He was on his back and there were hard, sharp things under him. It was uncomfortable, no, painful, and he tried to move but a wave of dizziness and nausea hit him. He could feel blood on his face, coming from his head, and knew that couldn't be good.

He lay still and took a deep breath but that hurt as well. He was pinned down, his legs immobile and something heavy was across his chest. He tipped his head, trying to see, and realized it was masonry from the shop.

Woolworths had gone. In its place was a huge, rubble-filled crater.

Fire was just starting to take hold and the dust was still thick but, as the air cleared, the scene revealed was one of horror.

Death and destruction.

Bricks and glass, flames and filth.

Blood.

Horror.

Death.

He tried to focus more closely, his head spinning, then inhaled sharply as he realized what he was seeing on the ground, just in front of him. It was part of one of the ladies that had been discussing wool just moments before. Part of her. He recognized her coat. The cuffs. Her hand lying bloodied in the dirt. The stitching at the top of the shoulder.

A corner of the collar and no more.

The bile rose in his throat and he forced it back down.

The other woman's foot and lower leg lay nearby.

Her stocking was torn and the sole of her shoe had been recently mended.

Slowly, without realizing it at first, the ringing in his ears decreased to a more tolerable level and he could hear other noises beside those in his head.

The roar of the flames, the sound of brickwork collapsing.

The tormented, desperate screams.

The pitiful cries for help.

"Help me," came an elderly man's voice. "Please, someone help me."

Bobby tried to move, ignoring his pain. He wanted to help, he needed to, but only one arm was completely free. He couldn't just lie there and listen to the suffering. He was a man of action, one who helped when others needed it.

The screams he felt all around him, inside his head.

The boom of the explosion, the pressure on his chest. He couldn't breathe, couldn't think.

The screams.

Almost inhuman, unreal.

The screams.

"Mummy." He heard it through the noise — a young child, a boy. Bobby looked round for him.

He was about seven or eight and trapped as securely as Bobby, his mother's dead body pinned under him. "Mummy," the boy said again, and Bobby reached out his free hand toward him.

"It's okay," he said. "It's all going to be okay. Look at me."

The boy stared over. He had thick, dark blond hair like Lewis'. It was messy and sticking up at odd angles, just like Lewis' did when he took his flying helmet off. There was blood on his face — blood and dirt and...a burn mark.

Bobby had seen burns before.

He hadn't been able to help Lewis when he was hurting. He had to do something now.

The boy's gaze bored into him, clinging on and holding him so Bobby couldn't turn away. And still the screaming went on. But the boy needed to look at him. Better he looked at Bobby than his dead mother or the body parts strewn all around him. If he looked at Bobby then he would be all right.

If only the screaming would stop.

If only Bobby could do something to help.

"Look at me," he repeated. He couldn't tell what his own voice sounded like, not with the noise in his head, but he had to do something. "Talk to me, and it'll all be okay."

But it wasn't okay. It was never going to be okay.

Over the next few hours, while the emergency services assessed and dealt with the more severely injured casualties first, Bobby talked to the boy then watched helplessly as he slowly slipped into unconsciousness and died.

Little by little, one by one, the screaming stopped and Bobby couldn't help any of those people either.

* * * *

One moment Bobby would have sworn he was asleep and thinking of nothing, the next he could feel the pressure of the explosion on his chest and the screaming started again. He could tell it was daytime by the light filtering through his eyelids but something wasn't the same. He was on his back but it was soft under him. He ran his fingers over what should be the ground and felt cotton. He tried to move his leg and it slipped easily.

The relief hit him like a double whiskey on an empty stomach as a wave of nausea rolled over him. He wasn't trapped anymore, he wasn't there, caught under the remains of Woolworths with brown wool and bits of body in front of him and... So why could he still hear screaming?

He tried to control his breathing and forced himself to open his eyes.

A bed with white sheets and a dark blanket. White walls, other beds, other people in the beds. People with bandages.

Hospital. He was in hospital, and bits of him hurt but it wasn't him screaming.

He looked around. Some of the men were asleep, one or two were walking along the ward, but most were lying in their beds reading, talking or just watching the world go by. Many were in pain but he couldn't see anyone screaming.

Only he could still hear it, the cries of people in pain, dying.

He realized his hands had balled into fists and his heart was beating faster. He could feel the pressure again on his chest, in his head.

Control.

He needed to get control.

He found a dark stain on the white wall opposite and stared at it. He had to control his breathing, slow it down, make it regular.

A long breath in and then out.

Repeat.

Remember that he was here in the hospital, not trapped, free to move around. Not pinned down by the front of Woolworths, staring at the mutilated arms and legs of middle-aged women as a young boy died in front of him and he did nothing to help anyone and… Breathe.

Don't think, just breathe.

Think of Lewis and flying. Soaring through the air with Lewis at his side, the water lost far below. Lewis with his long legs and thick hair. Blond hair, just like… Breathe.

Don't think, just breathe.

He stared at the spot harder, counting each breath in and out, bringing his mind back to the stain every time it wandered. But that wouldn't do, he had to think.

Lewis in the mess hall, pleading for coffee when all that was available was a never-ending supply of tea. Lewis and his not-so-secret love of British warm beer. Lewis' excitement each and every time they took off. His own excitement at a new piece of navigational equipment. The discipline and pleasure of successfully plotting a difficult route with inadequate maps. The expression on Lewis' face, in bed, after he'd come.

He could push away everything else that clouded his mind with that one image alone. That image could ground him and keep him in control.

He had to control his breathing and think of Lewis.

He made a conscious effort to flatten out his palms against the mattress as he plotted the outline of the stain. It could be an island in an old atlas or a treasure map with X marks the spot. After the war, soon, Lewis and he could go and dig up the treasure. They'd be rich. Rich enough to buy Lewis a Mosquito so he could fly to his heart's content forever and Bobby could sit by his side as they had adventure after—

A crash of sound.

Metal hitting something hard.

Loud, so loud.

Ringing in his head, making it hurt.

Shouts of...something. Hard, loud voices raised high.

Pressure on his chest, in his head.

The noise. Shouting. Screaming?

"Mummy." Was that real or in his head?

Pressure, pressure, noise.

The next thing Bobby was aware of was an elderly man in a white coat, crouching down in front of him. The man had his hand out toward Bobby but he wasn't trying to touch him. The palm was partially raised as though to reassure him, to support him. He was speaking slowly, his voice pitched low and his tone calm. He was repeating something. Bobby needed to concentrate, needed to hear what was being said. But why was the man crouching on the floor? Why didn't he stand next to the bed?

Because Bobby wasn't in bed anymore.

He was on the floor, squatting with his back pressed as hard as he could get it against the wall, squashed in between the bed and the battered bedside table.

He had no idea how he'd gotten there.

The man was speaking again. Bobby knew it was important that he listened. Important that he calmed his breathing down again and stopped looking like a mad man.

One thing at a time.

Calm his breathing then listen and maybe the last thing on his list would come automatically. He counted through a couple of breaths, taking his time, concentrating on the air in his lungs. Now listen.

"It's all right, son. You're all right," the man said.

Was he all right? He did a quick review of his body. There was pain but he wasn't quite sure where it radiated from. It didn't matter because he couldn't concentrate on the pain through the noise in his head and the pressure on his chest.

"You've had a nasty experience. You were caught up in a bomb blast." The man paused, as though giving Bobby time to absorb the information, or maybe to assess his reaction.

Bobby knew all about the bomb.

"You were one of the lucky ones. They're saying there are over a hundred and fifty dead but you're going to be fine." Again he paused and Bobby tried to think. A hundred and fifty dead. Two middle-aged, ample-bosomed ladies, one little boy, his mother and— Yes, he was lucky.

"But you have quite a severe wound to your head and lacerations across your legs. We need to get you back into bed. We don't want your stitches to be pulled open, do we?" The man waited and Bobby looked around him.

He couldn't remember why he was on the floor.

Something must have registered on his face because, when he spoke again, his voice was lower still and even more calming. "I'm Doctor Evans and you can trust me. I'm telling you you're going to be just fine. You've had a bad shock and, just when you needed a little quiet to adjust, one of the other patients knocked a tray of tea out of the orderly's hands. The noise made you jump but you're going to be fine. Everything is going to be fine. Do you understand?"

Bobby stared into the doctor's face. He had small round glasses with wire rims and lots of wrinkles in his skin. He was old and old people had experience, they knew things. The doctor said he was going to be fine.

Bobby nodded.

"Righty ho, there's a good chap." Dr Evans nodded and gave Bobby a smile, before talking to the nurses gathered behind him. "Let's get Squadron Leader Davenport back into bed. Then maybe we can think about finding him somewhere a bit quieter. Perhaps one of the smaller wards would be better for him and give him somewhere to think things through." He glanced back at Bobby. "Would that be a good idea?"

Again Bobby nodded. But maybe he needed to speak, if he was going to stop looking like a mad man. "Yes." His throat felt wrong—dry and painful, as though he'd been shouting—and his voice didn't sound right. "I'd like that. If it's possible."

"We'll see what we can do." Dr Evans helped him to his feet but Bobby knew it was important that he stood alone. He was a Squadron Leader, after all. A sudden wave of dizziness hit him, followed by a flash of pain in his head so bad he had to fight to breathe through it.

"Into bed," Dr Evans said briskly, and Bobby was bundled back into bed and the sheets smoothed out over him. "Let's give him something for the pain and then something to eat. I know a good strong cup of tea will make him feel much better and then we can sort out moving him. We need all our capable officers at their best."

Tea. Maybe it would help because the doctor was right. The last push of the war effort really did need everyone. "Thank you," Bobby said. Then he asked the most important question the best way he knew how. "Does my squadron know? My pilot?"

"Yes. After we sorted you out we got in contact with the RAF and they passed on a message to your people. We can't have them thinking you're AWOL or missing. I know one of your chappies wanted to come down and check on you but it's a long way from Lincolnshire, I'm not sure if that will be possible."

Someone wanted to come down and see him.

Lewis.

Bobby settled himself back against the pillows and let the thought wash over him. If anybody could find a way, Lewis would. It might not be today, or any time soon, but Lewis would be here and everything would be better. Bobby pushed the sound of the screaming away and concentrated on that thought.

* * * *

Bobby counted the rolled up bandages on the shelf opposite his bed. There were forty-seven. Two fewer than yesterday. He wondered who they had been used on, what their injury might be. The thought had him scratch at the wounds on his legs. They were healing and had gotten to the stage where they itched all the time. But he'd been told repeatedly to leave them alone, so he deliberately pulled his hand out from under the sheet.

Breathe, keep calm, don't let anything bother you.

Lewis was coming today. Hopefully. He'd been expected yesterday but that had fallen through after an unexpected raid to Germany. But he would be here today because he was going to see RAF Command to get the orders Bobby had so spectacularly missed.

Lewis would be here. Hopefully. All Bobby had to do was stay in control until he got here. He ignored the pain in his head and the distant sound of screaming and counted the boxes of dressings next to the bandages on the shelf. Eleven, twelve, thir—

"Bobby!" Lewis stood in the doorway, filling it not only with his sheer size but also with his energy, his enthusiasm. His smile was about a million miles wide and his eyes shone. "You're okay. I mean I knew you were, you said so on the telephone, but it's different, seeing you here, now, all...okay and alive and... It's good to see you." He suddenly seemed to become aware of the men in the other three beds in the room. "It's good to see you alive, Squadron Leader Davenport."

"Good to see you too," Bobby said. He was suddenly aware of a stinging in his eyes. God damn it, he was not about to cry, he never cried. He had to stay in control, had to.

The smile on Lewis' face faltered and he looked at Bobby a little closer. "You are okay, aren't you?"

"Yes." Bobby nodded and plastered on a smile. "I'm fine, just like the doctor said I would be."

"Okay." Lewis mirrored his nod then came over to the bed, pulling up a chair so he could sit tucked up in the corner, next to the window. "Now tell me how you're actually doing? What have the doctors done and what happened?"

Bobby sat up a little more and angled his back to the rest of the small ward. "One question at a time." He fixed on the shape and color of Lewis' eyes and ignored the pressure and noise in his head. "I told you what they did. I've got hideous black and blue bruises on my legs and back, plus some stitches. There's a bit of a hole in my head but they sewed that up as well, and I don't think any of my brain fell out."

"How bad is it?" Lewis asked.

Bobby shrugged. "I can remember what day it is and my name, unlike some poor bastards in here. I've been plotting routes to Berlin, just to see if I can still do it, and I've had no problems with the calculations. I'm okay, or I will be once it heals. It won't stop us flying."

"Good." Lewis smiled and squeezed Bobby's wrist, holding on a little longer than he should, before brushing imaginary crumbs off the sheet. "You scared the ever living shit out of me. I thought—" He laughed, although there was no humor in the sound. "No, you don't want to know what I thought. Let's just say it was pathetic, I was pathetic. We didn't know what happened at first. We got a message from Command saying you hadn't turned up for the meeting but no one knew where you were. I didn't know what the hell to do so I kept ringing HQ and our old bases. I even rang the train stations before starting on the hospitals."

"But I thought the doctor informed the RAF?"

"No one told us for three days. They were quick enough to say you'd missed the meeting, but didn't think it important to tell us you were hurt. They knew where you were so why bother telling us? Fucking idiots. It was only because I was making such a fuss that they got in touch."

"Three days? Shit." Bobby could imagine too well how Lewis had felt. He remembered the feeling from after Lewis' plane had crashed.

"Worse still came when I eventually did what I should have done straight away and contacted Bruce. He was farther away when the bomb went off so only had a few cuts and bruises. But he'd seen the destruction it caused, knew there were an awful lot dead. When he told me that I—" Lewis looked away and squeezed Bobby's wrist again. "I'm fucking glad to actually see you," he said softly. "So fucking glad." His voice dropped to a whisper. "I've never been so fucking scared in my life, I—"

Lewis stopped talking and pressed his lips hard together before looking back at Bobby. "But you're here and alive and so am I and everything is going to be okay." The smile he gave was real, even though it wobbled round the edges. "So tell me, what happened?"

Bobby forced a smile in return. "One minute I was waiting for a bus outside Woolworths—the next, half the storefront was on top of me."

"But you're really all right?" Lewis asked, and Bobby understood the need for endless reassurance.

"Yes, like I said, I'm going to be fine. There's no permanent damage."

"Thank God." Lewis nodded. "So tell me more."

"There's nothing else to tell. When the ambulances arrived they checked over who was in most need of help and dealt with them first. My injuries weren't life threatening, so I had to wait a little longer for the rubble holding me down to be cleared. But it was all done much more efficiently than I'd expected. I guess the British have had a lot of practice by now and the fire brigade and everyone else worked well together."

"Good for them," Lewis dismissed it. "Now tell me about you. How long did you have to wait?"

"I don't know." Bobby tried to think back. "It felt like forever but also a heartbeat and—" He shook his head, not really understanding why.

"What was it like?"

"It was... I'd been watching two ladies. They had old-fashioned hats on—one was gray with a felt flower. I could see them talking through the window pane and then it was gone and they were gone. But not gone because there were bits of them and... There was a boy and I tried to talk to him but I couldn't hear him properly, not through all the screaming. It went on and on and there was pressure and I couldn't do anything to help."

Bobby suddenly became aware of a stinging pain around his wrist. He stared down. Lewis was gripping him tightly, digging his fingernails into the delicate skin. He looked up and Lewis' eyes were full of concern. "Bobby," Lewis said softly, and Bobby thought he might have said it before. "You're not all right, are you?"

"I am. I told you, the doctors stitched me up and soon I'll be good to go."

"But you're not all right." This time it wasn't a question. "You have to tell the doctors."

"Tell them what? Tell them that I feel bad because I couldn't help? There must be millions of people that feel like that. Tell them I keep thinking about it? Of course I should think about it, it's only right for those people that died that someone remembers. Tell them I can't get the screaming out of my head? I—" He stopped, abruptly aware that he'd said more than he intended.

"Yes," Lewis said quietly, as he discreetly stroked the skin he'd just scratched. "Tell them all that. But most of all tell them about the screaming."

"No, I can't. I'll be fine. I just need a bit of time, that's all. A bit of time to sort it out in my head and then I'll be just fine. Have a little faith in me."

Lewis sighed. "You're going to be a stubborn bastard about this, aren't you?"

"Come on, you know me. If I say I'm fine I am. Now, tell me what they said at RAF HQ? Where are they posting us?"

Lewis sighed again and sat back. "They're not. Not for a while anyway. They're waiting to see what happens with you, if you're declared fit to fly again."

"When I'm declared fit to fly, not if," Bobby interrupted, and Lewis stared at him for a moment.

"They're going to wait and see what the situation is. Meanwhile I stay in Lincolnshire, which is too fucking far away from you here."

"It won't be for long, I promise."

"Bobby, don't rush it. You need to mend properly."

"And the RAF needs all the Master Bombers it can get to finish the war. I'm fine, I told you. Now tell me what's been going on back at base? Did they get the new directional equipment fixed?"

For a while they talked about familiar things and people and Bobby felt on safe ground. Slowly the pinched, worried look on Lewis' face started to smooth away, especially when Bobby started to talk heatedly about the new Oboe aerial targeting system.

Bobby felt confident and sure of himself. The screaming dimmed until it was just a murmur in the back of his mind. With Lewis next to him he knew that he was fine and that they could go on doing their jobs for the war effort.

"Have they given you any idea how long they're going to keep you here?" Lewis asked.

"Another week, I think. They need the bed and there's no reason to keep me any longer. I'm only here now because it's too far to go home to recuperate until I get back to full fitness. They said I need taking care of." Bobby pulled an annoyed face.

"I'll take care of you." Lewis didn't seem the least bit annoyed. "I'd like to do that."

"I think you'd like it a little too much." Bobby couldn't help laughing.

"And I'd make sure you'd enjoy it just as much. Tell them to release you back to base and then the doctors up there can decide if you're fit to fly. That's if I haven't worn you out first."

"Worn me out?" Bobby raised an eyebrow.

"In the nicest possible way." Lewis grinned. "I'm going to—"

But Bobby didn't hear any more. Without warning people started shouting in the corridor outside. They weren't cries of pain—this was voices raised in argument. But the unexpected noise broke Bobby's concentration.

Next thing he knew the screaming was back at full volume in his mind and he could feel pressure, pressure, pressure on his chest and in his head. For a moment he fought both to breathe and to remember where he was. He could see a foot with no leg and hear a little boy calling for his mother.

Control.

He needed to stay in control, to show everyone that he was fine.

He couldn't have a doctor see him like this or he'd never be declared fit to fly. No, he needed to calm down, focus and appear normal because there was a job to do, an important one, and in a moment he'd remember what it was.

Bombs.

No, not bomb, or not just bombs. Flying. Winning the war. Flying with...

He looked over and saw Lewis.

Lewis' mouth was forming Bobby's name, although he couldn't seem to hear it, not over the noise in his head.

Control. Focus and control. Be calm. Be normal.

He pushed the screaming and the pressure away and focused everything he had on Lewis.

It worked. A few moments later he could hear Lewis' concerned voice, feel where he was rubbing the back of Bobby's hand. Without any extra effort the volume of the screaming fell even lower and all Bobby could see was the small hospital ward and Lewis.

With Lewis there, control was so much easier.

"You're not all right. Please don't lie to me and say you are."

"I'm not crazy," Bobby blurted out breathlessly.

"Of course you're not, but you're not well either." Lewis leaned forward, studying him.

"I—" Bobby took a deep breath then another. "I can't have them saying I'm crazy."

"They aren't, not yet, you're too good at hiding it. But I know you too damned well for that. You went white and looked like you were in some kind of daze, like you weren't here anymore."

"But—" Again Bobby took a moment to think, to get back in full control. "I can't have anyone thinking I'm mad or they'll put me away somewhere and I won't be allowed to fight anymore. I have to fight, this war is too important not to fight."

"You've done your part. Someone else can take over for a while so you can—"

"No." Bobby knew he was nearly shouting and took a deep breath while he got himself back in check. "I started at the beginning and I'm going to make it to the end of the war. The only way I'm not is if they kill me. You know how important this is to me."

"Yes, I know," Lewis said softly. "But I also know how important you are to me. Your health comes first, before the war."

"Nothing comes before the war." But Bobby knew that wasn't an argument he could win, not with Lewis. He thought for a moment. "If they won't declare me fit to fly then we'll be separated and you'll get a new navigator."

Lewis' face closed up. They had flown apart and still did, but as rarely as they could possibly arrange it. Although it was never spoken about, every time one went up in the air without the other, Lewis would get tense and literally count down the time until they were both safe on the ground again.

Luckily, although both were good at their jobs, they were even better when they were working together. RAF Command wasn't stupid. With results like theirs they were kept together. The fact that they were both still alive after all these years was testament enough to their skill. Bobby knew it was his ace card and the only one he had left to play.

"If they separate us now, and assign you someone different, you know there's very little chance we'll be put back together, especially if we're as close to the end of the war as people are saying." He waited, giving Lewis time to work it out.

"But you're not right."

"I know but I will be."

"You have shell shock or combat exhaustion or you just need time to get over this."

"I know. I know what it's called and I know I could do with a bit of time but there isn't any. We're needed now, not in a few weeks. But I am all right," he went on quickly at the sight of Lewis' skeptical look. "I will be all right and it's so much easier when you're around." That he could say honestly and with heartfelt conviction.

Lewis must have read his thoughts on his face. "Really?"

"God, yes. Just having you in the room makes such a difference. You calm me, help me to focus."

"If that's true then what the hell are you like when I'm not here?" Lewis' voice rose.

"Shhh." Bobby waved him quiet, only too aware of the other men in the room. "I do okay. I am okay. It's just so much easier with you here. Think about it—if I'm declared fit to fly and we go back to normal, then you'll always be with me, especially up in the air." He could see Lewis wasn't convinced. "With you I can do anything, you know that. Without you… It's going to be fucking harder. Plus I won't be doing anything useful and you get a new navigator and we both know how you feel about that."

Now all he could do was wait for Lewis' reaction.

Lewis exhaled hard, went to speak then stopped, staring at Bobby. He shook his head and grimaced. "I don't like this one little bit. You need help now, they can do things to get you through this."

"But that takes time. Lots of it."

"I know, and I know you, you're desperate to do your bit. If they won't let you fly you'll only discharge yourself and drive an ambulance or man a gun emplacement down at Dover. I—" Again Lewis shook his head. "I'd rather have you where I can see you, where I can help, than off on your own. But if there's any sign, any sign at all, that you can't manage or you're getting worse then I'll drag your stupid ass to the doctor's. I'll even knock you out to get you there if I have to."

"You won't," Bobby said seriously. "I'm not stupid." He looked at Lewis seriously. "Good navigation is essential to the Pathfinders' work, even more so for a Master Bomber. If I get something wrong then the consequences could be horrendous. I won't, can't have that on my conscience. I promise you, if I can't do my job to my standard then I'll stop."

"You don't have to promise me because that's one thing I'm sure about. You're your harshest critic. You'll stop if it's the right thing to do."

"So you agree that I'll try and get out of here as soon as possible? That we go back to flying? That you'll help me?"

"Of course I'll help you and... Okay, we fly." He held up a hand as though to stop Bobby's smile of excitement. "We give it a try. A couple of test flights and then, if they go well, we try an operation. Any problems and we stop. Agreed?"

"Agreed." Bobby nodded.

"I just want you fucking well, that's all that matters to me. You need help now."

"It's not all that matters to me and I'll get help, if I need it, after the war is over."

"Sooner rather than later."

"After the war. Although I'm telling you I'm going to be fine."

"I just hope you're right."

* * * *

A week later Bobby was discharged from hospital. Much to his secret relief, Lewis was able to come down from Lincolnshire to travel back with him. He wasn't sure he was ready for a long, crowded train journey on his own. But Lewis being down meant that he was also there when the doctor finally let him go.

"You think he's ready to go back to work?" Lewis asked, as Bobby glared at him.

"He's done very well. The stitches are out and everything is healing nicely," Dr Evans said.

"But back to operational duty? You need to be more than stitch free for that."

The doctor took off his glasses, folded his hands on the desk and spoke to Lewis directly, ignoring Bobby as though he were not in the room. "RAF Command has left me in no doubt as to how valuable your Squadron Leader is to the war effort. He says he's fit and I know he is mostly healthy. What would you have me do?"

"I don't know," Lewis blustered. "I just want what's best for him."

"Perhaps you are concerned about your own safety and would prefer a new navigator. I'm sure that could be arranged."

"No, absolutely not. He's the best there is."

"And you are happy to fly with him?"

Lewis nodded.

"Well then, I release him back to the RAF in Lincolnshire. I'm sure you — they — will take good care of him."

Lewis pursed his lips and sat back. Everyone in the room knew where a conversation like that could go and Bobby was glad that Lewis didn't push it any further.

They caught the train a few hours later. And if Bobby jumped a little when there was an unexpected loud noise or pushed too close to Lewis in the crowd, he was sure he'd covered it up so that no one else would notice. As the train pulled out of the station, he rested against the blackout curtain covering the window, closed his eyes and pretended to sleep. The rhythmic, repetitive noise of the wheels on the track soothed his nerves and pushed the screaming down to an indistinct undertone.

* * * *

A week later Bobby was declared medically fit to fly by a doctor that hardly even glanced at him. He did read the notes prepared by Dr Evans, studying the recommendation carefully, then signed the paperwork without raising his head. Then they were back in the air.

Lewis insisted that they go up for a trial flight before they went back on operations but it wasn't needed. The air above Lincolnshire was free of any hostile threats and the cloud cover was slight. They soared, they pushed the engines to maximum speed, they flew low over familiar ground. Lewis, not so subtly, tested Bobby's navigation, but again it wasn't needed. Up there, with the freedom of space all round him, Bobby felt calm, practical and efficient. The horrors that plagued him at night fell away and he could breathe easier.

"It might be different in the dark," Lewis said as they taxied back across the airfield. "We should try it."

Bobby kept his fears to himself. The dark could be a difficult place. But flying was different from lying in bed, staring at the ceiling with nothing to occupy his mind except the effort of keeping thoughts at bay. When they were flying he was busy, there was work to do, and if there wasn't there was always Lewis to talk to. Up in their plane, just the two of them, he felt as confident as he ever had.

He tried to ignore the nagging voice in his mind that said practice flights were easy without bombs going off, enemy aircraft and ground guns trying to shoot them down.

When the Wing Commander assigned them their first mission, Bobby had to work hard to stay focused as the details were explained. He would be acting as navigator and Squadron Leader but it was a small operation, with no need for a Master Bomber.

As they came out of the briefing room Lewis moved closer so that no one else would hear their conversation. "Are you ready for this?" he asked. "It's no bad thing to say you need more time."

But Bobby knew time wouldn't make any difference. Whenever he did it, his first operation would still be as scary. He thought he might as well get it over and done with. "I'll be okay," he said, trying to convince both of them. "I'm fine."

Lewis stared at him, his lip caught between his teeth, and shook his head. "That is so visibly a lie and you're so clearly not fine it's almost funny."

"I am fine," Bobby tried to say but Lewis just continued to stare. "Is it that obvious?" He looked around him, conscious of the other crews. Crews he would be leading into hostile territory very soon.

"No." Lewis seemed to take pity on him. "It's not obvious. Even if the authorities weren't so desperate for good navigators that they ignore what's right in front of them, you're too good an actor and that stubborn, formidable willpower of yours keeps you too in control for anyone to notice. Anyone except me."

"And will you fly with me?"

"Yes," Lewis said simply. "I'd rather have you by my side than anywhere else and you're still the best."

"Good. Then let's get this show on the road." Bobby headed for the lead aircraft and Lewis followed behind.

Bobby was fine through the long journey across Allied held territory. It wasn't until they encountered their first flak that he started to breathe more rapidly and had to concentrate harder. When an explosion went off too close to their tail, he could feel himself start to shake. The pressure was back, in his head and on his chest. It never quite went away but he'd learned to deal with it, to push it to a dark corner of his mind along with the screaming.

Scoop it all up and tie it tight. He'd practiced doing that whenever there was something loud or unexpected, or when there were too many people around for him to think.

Scoop it all up and tie it tight.

He tried to do it now but there was another burst of gunfire and another. Then he felt a hand squeezing his thigh, pinching just enough to let him focus on it.

Lewis.

Look at Lewis. Focus on Lewis.

"All right?" Lewis asked.

"Yes." Bobby gave a snort of derisive laughter. "No. But I will be."

"Sure?"

Another explosion almost caught the airplane next to them, making theirs shake. Bobby fixed his sight on Lewis' hand on the controls, his long fingers curled tight, the line of skin above his glove.

He wasn't sure if he could actually smell Lewis or if it was more that he associated all the smells inside the small cockpit with Lewis. Either way it made him concentrate on here, now, and Lewis.

Lewis.

"Talk to me. Anything. Talk about anything, just for a moment."

Lewis gave him a brief glance then started to go through the instructions they'd been given. Distances, aiming points, number of aircraft. Bobby only heard the first few then he concentrated on the sound of Lewis' voice.

It was all he needed.

A couple of deep breaths, the sound of Lewis, his smell, his presence, that was all Bobby needed and he was back in control and listening to the words.

He corrected Lewis' deliberate mistake and they both smiled.

Bobby was going to make it.

Suddenly he was sure he could control all the bad things for as long as he needed to get the job done. He wasn't going to quit unless he was dead. If that meant clinging onto Lewis then he figured it was no hardship.

With Lewis at his side he could make it through the rest of the war and do something useful.

"I'm going to be okay," he said, and for the first time in too long he meant it.

"Good." Lewis gave him a quick smile and turned back to his job.

With Lewis at his side he could do anything.

Epilogue

September 1951 The Old Sheep Shed, Behind Coral Bay, Crete

Lewis closed the door quietly, slipped off his shoes and made his way through the semi-darkness across the familiar room to open the window a little wider. A slight breeze caught the net curtain making it billow, the corner flapping for a moment. It wasn't a cold breeze, not even a cool one, but it did refresh him as it stroked around his face, bringing with it the smell of the sea and the carob trees. He sucked in a lungful of air, held it for a minute, then let it go slowly with a sigh of pleasure before pulling off the rest of his clothes and slipping into bed.

He inched his way across the mattress, holding up the thin sheet so he could slide under it, liking the way it gave the impression of privacy, of intimacy. He stopped when he reached the warmth of Bobby's back, curving himself round the long length of his naked body so they touched from calf to chest. He dropped a quick kiss on Bobby's shoulder then pressed his nose into the faintly damp skin and inhaled.

He knew Bobby wasn't asleep, knew he could never quite relax until Lewis was home. But he also knew Bobby would be uncomfortable admitting it, now, after all this time—and everyone deserved their armor.

"Hi," he said, kissing again. "Good day?"

Bobby yawned before reaching back to pull Lewis' hand across himself and linking their fingers together. "Yeah. I got all last week's paperwork up to date and even started on this week's."

"Wow, I'm impressed." Lewis slid his leg over Bobby's, pressing himself closer.

"You should be." Bobby pressed back. "You? How did you get on?"

"Perfect flying conditions. The high winds that were predicted never turned up and it was like a movie trailer all the way to the other end of the island and back, with the sun slowly sinking into the sea as we landed." Bobby relaxed under him with every press of skin on skin. Although Bobby's breath started to come in a faster, deeper pattern as Lewis extradited his fingers and pushed Bobby's leg up.

"You flew back in the dark?" There was a hint of concern in Bobby's voice.

"Yes, just like I've done a hundred times before." He pressed up, rubbing his hard cock into Bobby's flesh. "Just like you know I have. And every time I come back just fine and make another of my perfect landings."

"Perfect, my ass," Bobby snorted.

"Talking about your perfect ass…" Lewis let the words hang as he used his hands on Bobby, taking his time just like he knew was appreciated. He pushed the sheet off them and kissed over Bobby's shoulder, up the hard line of his neck, to just let his teeth rest against the curve of his ear.

Bobby's chest expanded and contracted as Lewis slid his fingers deeper, pressing in just the right place, pausing when he knew it would cause maximum effect. He could happily spend all night doing just this. Listening to the delicious noises they made, smelling the pre-ejaculate that was starting to flow, feeling the give of Bobby's muscles and, most of all, feeling Bobby let go and allow all his worries to go floating off on the meager breeze.

But, he smiled to himself, he also liked a bit more and he could tell Bobby would soon start to get impatient. He rolled Bobby further over so he was half on his belly, half on his side, and pulled his top leg higher, before pressing up against him. "Now?"

"About time," Bobby said, grumbling. He settled himself with one hand under the pillow and pushed his hips back, offering himself.

Lewis took the hint. He pressed in until he'd just breached the muscle and paused. The air in the room seemed to still as their breathing adjusted and fell into rhythm, just the way Lewis liked. He still hadn't quite got used to this, the luxury of time, of not having to keep one eye open and one ear listening for the sound of someone approaching. Of not being furtive or feeling scared. Here, in their ramshackle old sheep shed, they were comfortable in the knowledge that they would be left alone. No one would sneak up on the pilot and his shell-shocked former navigator. Everyone in their part of the island knew that Bobby didn't take well to surprises or loud noises.

Here they were free to fuck as slowly as they liked.

He felt Bobby exhale, just as he did the same, and knew that it was time. "Okay," he whispered into Bobby's skin before kissing him. Then he slid in on one long, unhurried slide until there was nothing between them but warm air and anticipation. He ran his hand across Bobby's belly, feeling the muscles flutter, and slipped under his cock so the head bumped across his knuckles.

"That's not fair," Bobby said, rocking back onto Lewis' dick and forward to get more friction on his own. But there was no heat in the words. They both knew it would come.

"Stop moaning. You want this instead?" He pulled almost all the way out, paused as they both caught their breath, then pressed in harder and faster. He did it again, without the pause, one continuous fluid motion that made him ache from the soles of his feet to the top of his head it felt so good. The feel of Bobby under him, around him, squeezing his dick, making him shake as he thrust deeper, was the only thing he could think about. The only thing that mattered.

Then there were blunt fingernails digging into his wrist.

"Whoa, slow down, buddy. I want this to last." Bobby sounded amused. Amused but demanding.

"You are so fucking bossy." Lewis took a deep breath and slowed his hips to an unhurried pace. "Remember, you don't out-rank me anymore."

Bobby started to rock in what felt like the perfect rhythm. "No. But you always did go racing off, way too excited, and I always got us where we needed to go."

Where they needed to go. If felt like Bobby was doing just that, setting the pace for a long, slow fuck that would take them right where they wanted — no, needed to go. Lewis took a deep breath and made a conscious effort to match him, sliding his cock in as Bobby arched back. On the first go he was slightly off time. The second was better, but the third had them both sighing with pleasure.

He levered himself up on one elbow and pulled his knees under him, just a little, so he had more leverage without losing the glorious skin to skin contact. His next thrust made Bobby groan, a noise that had Lewis biting his own lip. He couldn't let this go too fast — Bobby would never forgive him. He carefully angled the next few thrusts to give Bobby maximum pleasure but keep himself just the right side, just in control.

Bobby lifted his knee even higher then reached round to pull himself farther open, sighing and moaning and making all kinds of delicious noises as he did it. Now that just wasn't fair.

"Thought you wanted slow?" he asked, as he pushed in again, deep as he could.

"Changed my mind." The pillow muffled Bobby's voice but the message was clear.

"Why didn't you say?"

This time Lewis could feel Bobby's chuckle through his body. "Didn't need to. I know you. Know just what gets you going."

Lewis would give him that. Bobby could get him to do almost anything with a twitch of his hips. But two could play at that game. He gripped onto Bobby's waist, arching his fingers to anchor himself as much as to hold him in place, then upped the pace.

"Oh," Bobby groaned on the first thrust. Again on the second then Lewis didn't give him time to make individual noises as he moved faster, pressed deeper. He rested his forehead against the nape of Bobby's neck, his open mouth against the skin, and breathed in Bobby's smell.

"God," he whispered. He wanted to say, "I love you." Wanted to shout it out as loud as he could, but they didn't do things like that. Did do or say things like that, not often. Instead he let the sensations wash over him, gloried in them, and let himself go, fucking deep, but not hard—he'd never go too hard—until he couldn't hold it back any longer. With a shout of pleasure he came, biting down on Bobby's shoulder as he did so.

A few more quick thrusts and he was done for. He panted hard as Bobby reached back to squeeze his arm. Then Bobby was moving again, going for his own cock.

"No you don't." Lewis stopped him. He pulled out gently and rolled Bobby, none too gracefully, onto his back. "You might know me but I know you just as well. Know what you like. What makes you sleep real good."

He pushed Bobby's legs apart and slipped in between them.

Bobby threw an arm over his eyes, then moved it farther up so it rested on his hair. They both knew how Lewis liked to watch his face, even, like now, when he had his eyes shut.

Lewis grinned, but then felt his smile turn softer as he stared. Bobby was laid out like a gift meant just for him, arms up above his head, legs spread wide. His skin appeared gloriously tanned against the white sheet—those areas that Bobby would allow to be shown to the sun. His brown legs were almost funny with the line of his shorts clearly marked and his white feet. Bobby always wore shoes and socks, no matter how hot it was, just like the troops had worn in North Africa and the Far East, during the war. It never failed to make Lewis smile.

Brown face, brown arms and hands, even the tops of Bobby's shoulders were a light golden color, having caught the sun when they swam in the sea. Which was the only time he would take his shirt off. Lewis was never sure if it was modesty or an odd sense of solidarity that kept Bobby's top on. Lewis didn't take his own off, not when there was anyone else around to see his scars.

It made an…interesting picture. Patches of white, various shades of brown and a stripe of pink across the top of Bobby's nose that never completely tanned. Interesting and perfect. But it was more than how he looked that made it perfect. It was the way he seemed calm, almost tranquil, and completely at ease, spread out on the mattress. His limbs carelessly resting on the sheet, his chest rising and falling gently, his eyes softly closed.

Bobby was at peace with himself and the world around him and that was a truly wondrous thing. Lewis had wondered at times if he'd ever see it again. Not after the awful day, near the end of the war in Europe, that had come so close to changing everything.

When the V2 rocket had landed on Woolworths one hundred and sixty people had been killed and a hundred and eight seriously injured. The doctor had said that Bobby was one of the lucky ones. In the weeks after, Lewis had had to keep reminding himself of that fact. Being powerless when so many were in need, and there was so much to do, had seemed to bruise Bobby's very soul. After four weeks spent shaking with fear, whilst insisting to everyone that he was fine, he was declared fit to fly again. What he had really needed was rest, quiet, and help.

They had limped through the rest of the war, doing the job that was needed, whilst holding Bobby's symptoms at bay. Bobby had used sheer willpower — Lewis had kept him close. But his refusal to get help had made matters worse in the long term.

At the end of the war they were stationed in Burma, where the constant heat prickled and the insects made their presence felt. By the time they were given their discharge papers they were unsure what to do or where to go. Lewis knew that he had to get Bobby somewhere safe and quiet. That if he didn't, sooner or later Bobby would snap. It had taken him nearly four years to find a place where they could put down roots.

At first he'd thought about Bobby's old idea of an island in the Pacific. They were already halfway round the world — a little farther would make no difference. But they hadn't fit anywhere they tried. Some places were just too small for them to find the anonymity they needed. Others were disapproving, although they were always very discreet. They needed somewhere they could, as Bobby used to say, let people pretend they didn't know and turn a blind eye.

In a fit of desperation Lewis had taken them home to Texas. It had been a disaster. Not only had everyone looked at them differently but, when he'd stood in the living room and introduced Bobby, even his own mother's face had closed up in distaste. Bobby went to see his family on his own. It was a brief visit.

After that they'd gone back to England for a while. But the country was gray and cold, still in the grip of rationing and trying to rebuild. There was also nothing for them to do there and they didn't fit anymore.

Eventually they had taken a job flying a small plane out to the Greek Islands. Lewis persuaded Bobby to stay on there for a while by saying he wanted to get some sun on his scars. He didn't pull that trick often but sometimes it was needed and he knew Bobby would never refuse. It turned out that his scars didn't like the sun but the result was what he'd hoped for. They stayed long enough to be offered more permanent work.

A former Air Transport Auxiliary pilot, Barbara, and her Greek husband were setting up a small flying business both to help the islands recover from the war and to develop the tourist industry. If a traveler was coming to see the sights of antiquity, why not fly between the islands and see as many as possible?

It was a good plan, a sound one. They just needed some money to make it work. After a lot of thought, Lewis and Bobby had invested all their savings into buying a light aircraft and gone into partnership with them. It might not have been a Mosquito, and they might only have been acting as a taxi or haulage service, but it was flying and that was good enough for Lewis.

Trouble was there wasn't really a need for a navigator on most of the flights. Wasn't the need and it also meant that a spare seat—one that could carry a paying passenger—was taken up. It was Bobby that came up with the solution. Lewis would work as a pilot—he was the flying addict, after all—and Bobby would do whatever else needed doing. But there were limits. He couldn't be around large groups of people, hated the hustle and bustle of a market or busy shop, and broke out into a sweat if there was an unexpected loud noise.

But he was meticulous, methodical and hard-working. It turned out he was excellent as a bookkeeper and at running the office—the quiet office, in an old shepherd's hut near the airfield, a ten-minute drive from the equally old and wonderfully isolated sheep shed, behind Coral Bay, that they had made their home. Here they had finally become settled and Lewis intended to stay. Anywhere Bobby could completely relax was just fine by him.

And if Bobby flew with him whenever there was room and he felt like it, well, did life get any better than that?

So maybe their life since the war was different from the fantasy Bobby had once described. Maybe it was quieter and Bobby wasn't quite the same man he had been. Neither was Lewis. But they were both alive, which was a miracle in itself, and together, and nothing else really mattered. Lewis had all he wanted, here, now, laid out in front of him on an old white sheet.

Now, he knew, his smile was tinged with contentment.

"Are you going to sit there watching me all night?" Bobby asked, opening his eyes. "Is this part of your evil plan—stopping me coming and then watch me squirm?"

"You're not squirming. You know you can trust me and it's coming." Lewis had to laugh. Bobby was as in control as ever but they both knew they could trust each other. "I get us where we need to be as well."

Bobby's face turned a little more serious and a lot more affectionate. "Yes, you do. You got us here." They also both knew Bobby wouldn't have made it on his own, that Lewis had been forced to take charge for a while. Bobby reached down and stroked the hair off Lewis' forehead. Then he gave a lecherous grin. "So what are you going to do now?"

Again Lewis laughed. "Thought I might start with this." He leaned down and licked a long stripe up Bobby's still-hard cock. Bobby caught his breath and closed his eyes, so Lewis did it again. "Then I thought I might try this next." He kissed one of Bobby's balls then sucked it into his mouth. Bobby sighed so Lewis settled himself better between his spread legs and got ready to enjoy himself.

He took his time, using all his skills and his knowledge of what Bobby liked to best advantage. Sucking on the head, a hand round the shaft at the bottom and never pin Bobby's legs down. Yes, he knew how to really get to Bobby and, in a few minutes, Bobby was lifting up toward him.

Lewis dipped his head, taking down as much as he could comfortably, pulling off slowly before slowing increasing the pace. The tip of Bobby's dick rubbed against the roof of his mouth, filling, without gagging him, as he tightened his lips. A little faster, a little tighter as he slipped his hands under Bobby's ass to both grip it and lift it toward him. Bobby might like being in charge but this show belonged to Lewis.

He felt, rather than heard, Bobby sigh and give in to it.

Although his jaw had a hint of an ache in it, Lewis loved doing this. Loved the feel of Bobby's cock, as well as the sight and smell of it. He dipped again then pulled all the way off and let a large droplet of saliva run down the shaft. He knew just how much Bobby loved that, the feel and look of it, when he could concentrate long enough to look, and he was rewarded with a groan of approval. Then he sucked very gently on the head, letting his tongue map out the surface.

Now he could feel Bobby trying to hang on, trying not to thrust up into his face too hard. He knew Bobby would be repeating over and over to himself 'hang on just a bit longer, just a bit longer' like a mantra. He sucked again and could feel it starting to break Bobby, just like it always did. He blew a cold, long stream of breath right at the base of Bobby's saliva-slicked cock and watched him shake.

It wouldn't take long now.

Lewis pressed Bobby's thighs a little farther open and tilted them to the perfect angle before sucking his way back down as far as he could go. He tightened his lips and let them ride over the hard flesh on the upward journey as he walked his fingers toward darker places.

When he pushed inside, Bobby lost any semblance of control, his hips pushing up hard before sinking back onto the counter stimulation, and he came with a moan of appreciation. Lewis kept going. One, two more short spurts and Bobby was reaching down wildly, trying to find Lewis' hair. After a few missed attempts he caught hold, tightening the strands between his fingers.

Bobby pushed up again half-heartedly as he panted, and Lewis smiled around his mouthful, pleased with himself.

Bobby's grip loosened and he patted Lewis' head before flopping back out and exhaling hard.

Slipping off with a soft pop, Lewis wiped his mouth on the inside of Bobby's thigh then propped himself on an elbow to look up. "All right?" He smiled.

"God, yes," Bobby said. Then he suddenly laughed and reached down to pull Lewis up by his biceps, until they were tangled together side by side. They were contentedly quiet for a while until Bobby spoke again, his voice low and serious. "You know I really am all right, don't you?" He huffed out a short, dismissive-sounding breath. "I mean, I might not be quite who I was but I'm okay. Not quite the man you fell for but not so different, not... Sort of the same underneath. And all right. Not mad or bad but..."

Lewis rolled over and kissed him. "Shut up," he said with a smile. He knew how hard Bobby found it to have this sort of conversation. How hard and how he still felt he needed to explain or maybe even apologize. Lewis guessed that it would always be his job to convince him how unnecessary it was. "You're just the same as you always were. Same stubbornness, same principles, same integrity and the same stupid side that means you need me to make you see sense. Just the same as you always did. So you don't like crowds anymore. So what?" He grinned, as devilishly as he knew how. "That means I don't have to share you. I'm not complaining."

"We're really all right?" Bobby asked.

Lewis nodded and kissed him again. "All right and in it for the long haul."

"Good." Bobby breathed the word almost silently as he pulled Lewis in closer.

Lewis rested his head on Bobby's chest and ran a finger through the curled hair. "Plus, because I'm so good to you, I'll take you flying tomorrow. We could go to one of the other islands." He kissed Bobby's nipple. "Or maybe just up above the clouds, where it's only you and me."

Bobby sighed and Lewis felt him relax completely. Bobby really did love flying almost as much as he did.

Almost.

About the Author

When Faith was clearing out her attic many years ago, she found a book she'd written as a ten-year-old. On rereading it she realised that it was the love story of two boys. Over the years her fascination with the image of beautiful young men, coiled together as they fell head over heels in love, became a passion for her.

Since that first innocent book—written in purple sparkly pen—she has written many stories, set in varied worlds, but always with two men finding their way to happiness.

Still nothing much has changed because now she can be found in a daydream, wandering around the supermarket, or sitting in a meeting at work still dreaming up stories.

Faith Ashlin loves to hear from readers. You can find her contact information, website details and author profile page at http://www.totallybound.com.

Totally Bound Publishing